A GRIZZLY DOZEN

DOZEN

'12 TORTURED TALES FOR LOVERS OF SQUEAM'

WARNING

THIS BOOK IS DANGEROUS!
CLOSE THE COVER!

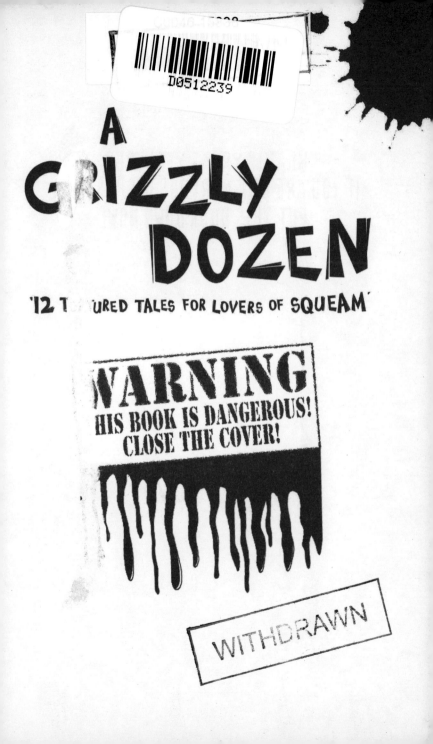

WHAT IS WRONG WITH YOU?
IF YOU ARE OF A NERVOUS DISPOSITION
PUT THIS BOOK DOWN NOW!

A GRIZZLY DOZEN

'12 TORTURED TALES FOR LOVERS OF SQUEAM'

JAMIE RIX

Illustrated by Steven Pattison

WARNING
THIS BOOK IS STILL DANGEROUS
CLOSE THE COVER

Orion
Children's Books

DO NOT OPEN THE DOOR!

(IF YOU ENTER)

THE DARKNESS

THERE IS NO GOING BACK

To Helen, Louisa and Richard

First published as two separate volumes – *Nasty Little Beasts* and *Gruesome Grown-ups*
in Great Britain in 2007
by Orion Children's Books
This edition first published in Great Britain in 2009
by Orion Children's Books
a division of the Orion Publishing Group Ltd
Orion House
5 Upper St Martin's Lane
London WC2H 9EA
An Hachette UK company

1 3 5 7 9 10 8 6 4 2

A catalogue record for this book is available from the British Library.

Printed in Great Britain by Clays Ltd, St Ives plc

ISBN 978 1 4440 0012 2

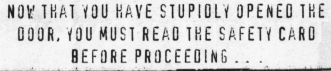

NOW THAT YOU HAVE STUPIDLY OPENED THE DOOR, YOU MUST READ THE SAFETY CARD BEFORE PROCEEDING . . .

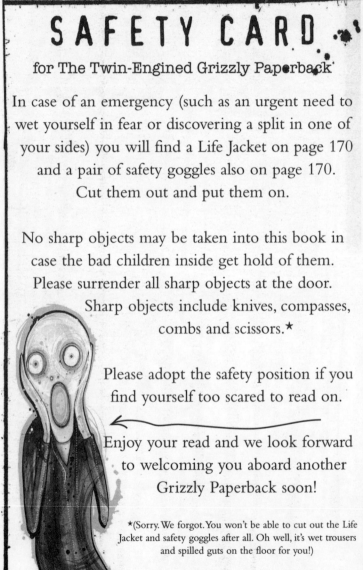

SAFETY CARD

for The Twin-Engined Grizzly Paperback

In case of an emergency (such as an urgent need to wet yourself in fear or discovering a split in one of your sides) you will find a Life Jacket on page 170 and a pair of safety goggles also on page 170. Cut them out and put them on.

No sharp objects may be taken into this book in case the bad children inside get hold of them. Please surrender all sharp objects at the door. Sharp objects include knives, compasses, combs and scissors.★

Please adopt the safety position if you find yourself too scared to read on.

Enjoy your read and we look forward to welcoming you aboard another Grizzly Paperback soon!

★(Sorry. We forgot. You won't be able to cut out the Life Jacket and safety goggles after all. Oh well, it's wet trousers and spilled guts on the floor for you!)

WELCOME TO
THE HOTHELL DARKNESS
BREAKFAST 7.30AM-9.30AM.

NO PARENTS UNLESS BY PRIOR
ARRANGEMENT WITH THE MANAGEMENT. IT IS OUR
JOB TO MAKE YOU FEEL AT HOME. IF THERE IS
ANYTHING WE CAN DO TO MAKE YOUR STAY
WITH US MORE UNCOMFORTABLE PLEASE DO
NOT HESITATE TO RING THE FRONT DESK. IT IS
MANNED DAY AND NIGHT BY A STUPID GIRL
WHO SNAPPED OFF HER ARMS WHEN SHE
STOOD UP AND WAVED OUT OF A CAR'S
SUNROOF WHILE IT WAS SPEEDING THROUGH A
TUNNEL; SO DON'T BE SURPRISED IF SHE
DOESN'T PICK UP.

The Night-night Porter

Hello. You came.

I've had my eye on you ever since you picked up the book. Luckily I've got my eyeballs in today. Some mornings I am in such a hurry to get to work that I forget to put them in. On such days I rely on my nose. It can smell a BAD CHILD at a thousand paces. You're a bit niffy, but I like that in a guest.

Were you worried that I wouldn't have any vacancies? Don't be. There are always vacancies at The Hothell Darkness. I keep a room for every child in the world. Your name is already on the door.

You'll like your room. I designed it myself. It has fresh crocodile-skin sheets, a mini-bat, scare-conditioning and hot and cold running cockroaches. Very shriek-chic.

You may not know who I am, but I know who you are. I even know where you USED to live. Would you mind if I asked you a few questions? Nothing too hard. I just want to check that you are beastly enough for The Darkness!

ANSWER TRUTHFULLY!

1) Have you ever told a lie? *Answer yes, because 'no' will be a lie.*

2) Have you ever laughed at an animal caged at the zoo? *They deserve it, don't they?*

3) Have you ever left food on the side of your plate? *I know I have!*

4) Have you ever slept the wrong way up in your bed? *Naughty, naughty!*

5) Have you ever shouted loudly near an old person? *Tut tut.*

6) Do you sometimes wish that your parents would put their heads in a food blender and leave you alone? *Haven't we all.*

7) Do you eat with your mouth full? *You big pig!*

8) If you could bury the worst experiences of your life in a box to get rid of them, would your teachers be the first thing you put in? *That's right, nobody likes a teacher. Crabby know-alls!*

9) Are you smaller today than you will be tomorrow?

10) Have you ever stayed in a hothell before? *It doesn't matter. You're here now, that's all that counts. Please leave you parents' credit card at the desk.*

Well done! You are BAD and have failed with flying colours! You win an indefinite stay with me in The Darkness for ever.

I just know that you and I are going to have such fun together! Now that you are down here for ever, you must acquaint yourself with your fellow guests/prisoners/torture victims.* To help you get started I have selected a few of their personal stories from our Visitor's Book, or as I prefer to call it The Book of Grizzly Tales. These are their tales as told to me.

* delete where applicable

Boo hoo! Boo hoo!

Gurgle! Goo-goo!

Boo hoo hoo! Boo hoo hoo!

Squeak! Squeak! Splat!

Heeeeeeeeeeeee

A

WHAT DID YOU SAY? SPEAK UP! I CAN'T HEAR YOU ...

Oink!

Don't eat me again! Please don't eat me again!

Bubble, bubble, bubble

Dig-diggerdy-do!

eeeeeeeelp!

I wan—I wan—I wan—I w—

aaaaaaaaaagh! This is a nightmare!

Oink!

SHUT UP!

Honestly, those guests! Noisy bunch of ingrates. It's not enough that I feed them and change their water every week, they want to be let out as well! What do they think this is, an hotel?

Well, it is, of course. I know it's called a *hothell*, but really that's just an hotel with fiery pits. And very happy YOU'RE going to be here, too.

Now, the children in these first six tales live in the ANIMAL WING of the hothell, not because their evil minds are UN-STABLE, but because they all have one thing in common: they are all NASTY LITTLE BEASTS!

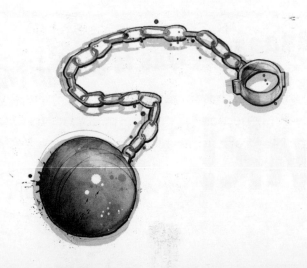

THE GRUB A-BLUB-BLUB

In sunny Skegness, in the Museum of Freaks and Oddities, in a glass case marked DO NOT FEED, lives the largest, laziest witchetty grub ever known to man. A witchetty grub, for those of you who've never eaten one, is normally the size of a corn dog. The one in the glass case is the size of a corn cow. It's big and fat with a body like stacked rubber tyres. It lives on a diet of pizzas, milkshakes and popcorn and occupies its time by watching the telly.

> Oh. I do love The Telly. It's to blame for so much bad behaviour!

The museum has nicknamed it the Grub A-Blub-Blub, because at night time it cries itself to sleep. Not surprising really, because it's not a grub at all!

* * *

Boo hoo! Boo hoo!

Let her cry! She's brought it on herself.

Savannah Slumberson was cursed. Not by trolls or bad fairies, but by her parents. They belonged to that select breed of adult who believes that life is best lived outdoors. Never a weekend passed when they weren't out scaling peaks or yomping through bogland or cycling the Pennine Way. They liked being cold and wet. They preferred their clothes sticky and damp. They looked forward to blisters and welcomed a wind-burn or three. If you asked Savannah's parents to choose between a weekend break in a posh hotel, or sleeping with badgers and digging a hole for a loo, they were hole diggers every time! Their hallway was a monument to the Great Outdoors, piled high with walking sticks, muddy boots and steaming woollen socks with that unmistakable tang of unwashed yak.

Savannah was cursed because her parents were

 ramblers and *she*, most definitely, was not. The furthest Savannah liked rambling was from the

warmth of her bed to the fridge. The closest she liked being to the weather was watching it on the telly or thumbing her nose at it through the window. Savannah was a lie-a-bed, a slovenly sloth, who despised everything her parents stood for and made it her daily task to do the exact opposite of whatever they wanted her to do.

※ ※ ※

Mornings in the Slumberson house always followed a similar pattern. Savannah would lie in while her parents rose with the lark and made preparations for that day's excursion. Then, at seven o'clock sharp, they would wake Savannah up by flinging back the curtains and opening the window. It was always a source of acute embarrassment when her parents tramped into her bedroom, coiled with ropes and crampons, wearing khaki shorts and hard hats!

'With a step and a stamp
And a heave and a ho,
It's a mighty hearty tramp
And a Ramb-er-ling we go!'

As they sang out of tune, Savannah pulled the duvet up around her ears.

'Oh come on, Savvy, sweetie!' pleaded her mother. 'You'll love it at the summit.'

'Summit!' yelled Savannah. 'What summit?'

'It's only a *little* mountain,' said her father.

'Do I look like a goat?' growled Savannah. 'Because you must be confusing me with something that LIKES it up mountains! Go away. You're depressing me!'

But Savannah's parents never went away. They just kept coming on like a bad dose of stomach cramps. If she locked her bedroom door and tried to stay in bed all day, they would attach grappling hooks to her window sill and climb up ropes to reach her. Then they'd knock on her window and whisper quietly through the glass.

'Oh, Savannah! Oh, Savannah, darling! It's time to get up!'

Which was why Savannah spent her whole life being never less than grumpy.

But thankfully that was all about to change! For the worse!

Boo hoo! Boo hoo!

Oh, do shut up and have another twelve pizzas!

✳ ✳ ✳

Back in March when the Slumberson family were choosing a summer holiday, Savannah had begged her parents to take her to a bed and breakfast in Bridlington where, for two whole weeks, she could indulge her twin passions for bed and breakfast. But her parents had a special treat for her instead.

'We're going on a camping holiday!' trilled her mother one morning. 'In a tent with sleeping bags.'

Her father's eyes were gleaming with excitement. 'It's going to be such fun. Cooking on an open fire, early-rising, cycling to—'

'*Cycling!*' Savannah was lying wrapped in her duvet on the sofa scoffing waffles when her father unleashed this latest surprise. The shock shot an unchewed lump of waffle down her windpipe and made her choke.

'Yes, cycling,' said her father. 'We're taking the bikes! Why else

would I have bought you these?' And he produced a plastic bag from behind his back. If there was one thing Savannah loathed more than cycling it was cycling lycra! Body-hugging, dog sick-coloured clothes that showed off every lump and body-bump.

'I am not wearing those!' she yelled. 'You will have to put me under general anaesthetic before I let you near me with a stitch of that!'

But parents being parents, with greater powers than even the police, they confiscated her television and said that they would recycle it in the river if she didn't do as she was told.

'I hate you,' seethed Savannah when she gave in. 'I'm only doing this because you're blackmailing me. Just because I'm coming with you this year does not mean that I shall ever be going on holiday with you again!'

A truer truth wath never spake!

* * *

 By seven o'clock the following morning, Mr and Mrs Slumberson were ready on the front lawn, standing astride their bicycles, which were

laden with rucksacks, cooking equipment, hurricane lamps, bedding rolls and a family tent. It was a six-hour ride to the campsite so they were keen to get going. Savannah had been dragged reluctantly out of bed, and had tried every trick in the book to be left behind: sitting on the loo for two hours, pretending to forget  her luggage fourteen times and suddenly feeling ill.

'I think it might be rickets,' she whimpered. 'Why don't you go on and I'll catch up when I'm better!' But her parents were having none of it.

'You're coming now!' shouted her father.

'It's not fair,' squawked his awkward daughter. 'I'm not even awake yet.'

'That's OK,' said her mother. 'The cycling will wake you up.'

'But … But …'

'What?'

Savannah wanted to say that the lycra made her look like a walrus and she wasn't coming, but she knew what her parents would say.

'Where we're going, Savannah, it doesn't matter what you look like. Sheep have no interest at all in how you look.'

This is untrue, of course. Some sheep are very snappy dressers. Others look like mutton dressed as lamb. 'Baa ha ha!' is the sound of a sheep laughing at lycra.

※ ※ ※

So off they went, but not before Savannah had pleaded cramp at the end of the road.

'Ow, it hurts!' she cried. 'Why does this always happen to me?'

'Take a rest and see how it is in a moment,' her father said stupidly.

'Jolly good,' said Savannah, wrapping herself up in her quilted sleeping bag and lying lengthways across her saddle and handlebars to get some long overdue shut-eye.

Savannah had got her way. Not only did she not have to cycle, but if she kept her eyes closed for the whole journey she would not have to see the appalled faces of passers-by when they heard her parents' embarrassing singing.

> *'Oh we're off on holiday,*
> *Feeling full of beans, let's play.*
> *Let's raise a cheer*

'Cause we're nearly there.
Hip, hip, hip, hip hooray!'

This was how they arrived at the camping site, not six but *twelve* hours later — Mr and Mrs Slumberson puffing up front with their lazy  'Gosh!-Have-I-really-slept-through-the-whole-journey!' daughter in tow. It was with a certain amount of horror, however, that Savannah opened her eyes for a quick peek at her surroundings and saw a sign pinned to a tree by the side of the track that led into the forest:

FIT CAMP

She didn't like the sound of that!

The campsite owner, Mrs Evadne Sprite (a bony woman of advancing wrinkles who liked to keep active) was juggling with three medicine balls outside her lodge. The Slumbersons introduced themselves.

'Welcome to Fit Camp,' Mrs Sprite said. 'Turkish wrestling for the over-eighties at five o'clock tomorrow morning. Anyone interested? Savannah?'

'Can human beings get up at five o'clock?' yawned Savannah. 'Doesn't it kill them?'

'No more than staying in bed,' chuckled the old lady. 'So I'll put your name down, shall I?'

'Certainly not,' said Savannah. 'I'm not over eighty.'

'And never will be by the looks of things.' It was a mysterious thing for the old lady to say and was met by a cold stare from Savannah. 'Camp rules are as follows. Everyone to have a good time and nobody to stay in bed beyond sun-up!'

'What sort of a holiday's *that*?'

'A healthy sort of holiday,' said Mrs Sprite.

'Ugh!' Savannah pulled her sleeping bag tightly around her shoulders.

'Seize the day, before the day seizes you!' snarled Mrs Sprite in a tone that sounded less like a friendly word of advice and more like a mortal threat.

Suddenly, a disgustingly fat larva, the size of a large lump of snot, fell out of the sky and landed on top of Savannah's head. She screamed as it wriggled on her scalp and tangled itself up in her hair. She slammed her cycling helmet back onto her head and felt the bug burst. Its innards dripped down behind her ears like warm lemon curd. She looked up and screamed again. There were thousands of them hanging off the branches of the trees like giant-sized jelly babies.

'What are those?!' she cried.

'Witchetty grubs.' The old lady smiled a toothless grin. 'Lazy little beggars. In this neck of the woods, if you stand still for too long they'll hitch a ride on you. That's why I keep my campers moving. One-two! One-two! There's less chance of being witchettied!'

Savannah did not like this place.

'Get our tent up!' she bawled.

Sensing a nightmare holiday in the making, Savannah decided that the best way to avoid the grubs and Mrs Sprite's exercise regime was to stay in bed and sleep for seven days. Her parents, however, had other ideas.

Every morning, with the dew still wet on the grass, they dragged Savannah out of her sleeping bag and took

her on a trip to some place of local disinterest.

They took her to an old church, and stood in the cemetery in the pouring rain admiring the slate roof and thick stone walls.

'It's amazing to think,' said her father, 'that this is an old Norman church.'

Savannah licked the rain off the end of her nose. 'It might be amazing to Old Norman,' she grumbled, 'but it's as boring as billiards to me. I want to go back to bed.'

They visited a Roman aqueduct and stood underneath its towering arches.

'I could stand here and look at this all day!' beamed her mother.

'Then you must be dead!' sulked Savannah, leaning her head against the aqueduct and closing her eyes. 'You're only allowed to wake me up if it moves.'

And they visited the only lawnmower museum in the world.

'Fascinating things . . . lawnmowers,' said her father, lifting his head from the museum guide.

'Absolutely,' said Mrs Slumberson. 'Is that a *Qualcast 35S* I see?'

'Of course you do know why this is the only lawnmower museum in the world, don't you?'

interrupted Savannah, as she struggled to keep her eyelids open.

'No,' said her father. 'Why?'

'Because lawnmowers are so blinking **BORING** nobody other than you two wants to look at them!'

But when Savannah's parents announced a trip to Shinwell's oldest Sewage Works, Savannah put her foot down.

'I am having a lie-in,' she snarled turning over in her sleeping bag, 'and there's nothing you can do to stop me!' And with that she disobeyed not only her parents, but also the rules of Fit Camp!

✹ ✹ ✹

Over by the office, underneath a canopy of trees, Mrs Evadne Sprite was eating her breakfast: a big bowl of live witchetty grubs. She picked up each grub by its head and bit off the back end from just below its neck. Then she threw away the head while it was still twitching. The shock of hearing Savannah shout '*I'm having a lie in!*' made her bite down too hard and she accidentally swallowed a grub whole.

> A witchetty grub's head is full of poison and Mrs Sprite was immediately sick. The pain in her stomach, however, was but a gnat's wince compared to the pain that now awaited Savannah!

That night, after Savannah had spent the entire day in her sleeping bag eating pizzas, Mrs Sprite came to the Slumberson tent and offered to take the girl's parents on a midnight bat walk.

SQUEAK! SQUEAK! SPLAT!

> You're not going anywhere, Cherie.

'You'll be away all night,' Mrs Sprite told them, when they jumped at the chance.

'Savannah,' said Mrs Slumberson, 'do you mind if we leave you on your own tonight?'

'Whatever,' said the lazy girl. 'I'm not bothered.'

'The sleep will do her good,' the old lady said sarcastically. 'Only make sure you stay inside your tent,' she warned her. 'When there is a full moon the witchetty grubs are restless.'

Savannah snorted with derision. 'If you think I'll be leaving my sleeping bag out of choice,' she said, 'you must be crackers.'

'But I'm *not* crackers,' cackled Mrs Evadne Sprite, which rather implied that Savannah would be leaving her sleeping bag whether she liked it or not.

Six hours later, still on her own, and with a full moon hanging high in the sky, Savannah was woken by a strange plopping noise outside. It sounded like heavy drops of rain exploding on a lily pond. She switched on her torch and flicked the beam across the sides of the tent, but could see nothing. More plops. She flashed the torch upwards and was horrified to see that the canvas roof of the tent was heaving. It had sagged in the middle and was nearly touching her head. She had to get out before it split and showered her with whatever foul things were up there!

Frantically gathering her sleeping bag around her for protection, she unzipped the front flaps of the tent and slithered out into the forest to see what was causing the bulge. Her blood froze. It was raining witchetty grubs! They dripped off the trees like thick slime and bounced off the tent's roof, using it like a trampoline to flip 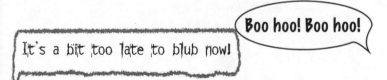 down the back of Savannah's neck and into her sleeping bag!

She did all she could to swat them off her skin. She screamed and threw herself back inside the tent. She tried to zip the flaps up to stop this invasion of sluggery, but thousands of grubs slithered through the opening and overwhelmed her. They cocooned her where she lay, binding her into her sleeping bag with a sticky gossamer web that closed her eyes and stopped her from screaming.

Then, with their work complete and the sun nearly up, they slithered slowly back to bed on the overhanging branches of the trees.

Boo hoo! Boo hoo!

It's a bit too late to blub now!

When Mr and Mrs Slumberson returned a few minutes later, their daughter was nowhere to be seen. They found a large, lazy witchetty grub inside the tent, which Mr Slumberson chucked out while Mrs Slumberson waved her arms and shrieked.

Then they left the camp site for good, vacating their lot for an outdoor family from sunny Skegness. It just so happened that the husband was the curator of a Museum for Freaks and Oddities!

And Mrs Evadne Sprite? She still takes her breakfast in the open air, under the canopy of trees. This morning she was singing a new song.

'Stitchetty twitchetty
Witchetty grub
Fat as a corn cow
And lacking in love.
Stitchetty twitchetty
Witchetty grub
In bed now for ever
So why do you blub?'

I've just had great news! The Museum for Freaks and Oddities is closing next year, because the cost of Savannah's pizzas has bankrupted them. When it finally shuts she's coming here. I've prepared Room 492.567 for her. I've called it The Kebab Suite. She can still watch telly all day, but she has to stand up to do it. It's not as cruel as it sounds. She doesn't have to support her own weight, because I'll be replacing her backbone with a high-tensile metal skewer. She'll never get bored, because I'll be constantly changing her view by turning her in never-ending circles. And she'll never get cold, because I'll be heating the room to 100 degrees centigrade with a stainless steel electric grill. The only thing I won't be doing is pizzas, not in The Kebab Suite. If she's hungry, I'll just give her some pitta bread and a bacon slicer and she can carve a bit of flesh off her own body!

The room next to Savannah's belongs to a devilish boy called Monty.

Heeeeeeeelp!

At least, the room would belong to Monty if Monty lived there. I've given him permission to live off the premises with a group of wicked children called The Sewer Rats. I'm not going soft. The place they live in is so vile and disgusting that there isn't a room in this hothell that can better it!

Now, all the children down here will tell you

that I KNOW EVERYTHING. So when I tell you facts you'd do well to listen. If I catch you NOT listening you'd better put a concrete roof tile in the seat of your pants. OK? Thwack Thwack!

To help you prepare for the arrival of my interesting facts I shall precede any announcement with this simple heading: NEXT—An Interesting Fact.

When you see NEXT—An Interesting Fact you should brace yourself for a dose of learning. I know you get enough learning at school. I know it makes you cross and badly behaved . . . and that's rather what I'm hoping for!

NEXT—AN INTERESTING FACT

On planet Earth 27,000 animal species become extinct every year. That's seventy-four per day, or to put it another way, ten species on each of the seven continents, which means that in Great Britain alone there is one species popping its clogs every week. I know which species died out this week. It's the little known Really Horrid Brother Called Monty Who Thinks It's Acceptable To Bully His Sister And Make Her Scream And Scream By Teasing Her With Exotic Pets Like Creepy Crawlies And Snakes species, which can generally be found at Brown Trouser Farm, Piddlepants on the Wold, Cheshire.

MONTY'S PYTHON

Monty was a bad boy. He was a home-based terrorist, who lurked in the shadows of the farmhouse where he lived, stalking his soppy little sister, Mayflower: chasing her, pinning her down and threatening her with all sorts of WOMD, otherwise known as Wrigglies of Mass Dread.

For example, if she was playing nicely in the buttercup meadow, building a fairy ring out of freesias and crocuses, Monty would sneak up behind her, and drop something sharp and hard down her back of her dress.

'Scorpion!' he'd cry.

To which Mayflower's response was predictably, '*AAAAAAAAAAGH!*'

Monty would then split his sides while his petrified sister, with eyes as big as porcelain door knobs, ran through their mother's flowerbed shredding her dress on the thorns. Only when Monty spotted his parents charging up the garden path did he hurriedly admit to his deception to shut his sister up. 'It's a carrot, you baby!'

When his parents weren't there, however, Monty's wicked teasing reigned supreme. His favourite time of day was bedtime. In the *dark*, a girl's imagination runs wild. Rarely did Mayflower go to bed without something cold and slimy brushing against her feet, and in the shadows a ghostly voice whispering in her ear. 'That's worms in your bed, that is!'

And Mayflower never gave anything less than a lung-bursting scream by way of reply.

'AAAAAAAAAAAAAAAGH!'

Only it was never worms in her bed.
'It's licorice!' sniggered Monty.

* * *

Mayflower had lost count of the number of times Monty had sprung out from behind the fridge at breakfast and thrown something glistening into her cereal.

'Ugh!' he shouted. 'Mayflower's a freak! She likes slugs in her cornflakes.'

In fact, he'd done it once too often. So much so that even Mayflower, the wettest fish in the bucket, stopped screaming.

'I'm not an idiot, Monty,' she sneered. 'I know they're not slugs. What are they really?' It never crossed her mind that Monty might be double-bluffing.

'Slugs!' he cried gleefully.

'*AAAAAAAAAAAAAAGH!*

At which point Mayflower rushed from the room to be sick, leaving Monty chuckling to himself and pondering his evil genius!

'They're marshmallow chunks!' he snickered cruelly. 'You big girl!'

But just as Mayflower grew weary of these games, so too did Monty. After years of teasing his little sister with pretend bugs and slugs her screams began to bore him. He needed a louder, more terrified response to keep his interest alive, and where better to turn, he thought, than pets.

Mayflower loved her pets; the cuddlier the better. She gave them soppy names, and told them lovely stories, and when they died she buried them in lace-trimmed cardboard shoeboxes. But Monty was not thinking cuddly. Cuddly was for *girls*. The pet he had in mind was beastlier by design!

✷ ✷ ✷

He bought his pet python from a pet shop. He went in with an empty carrier bag and came out with it bulging. The pet shop owner – a man with porcupine eyebrows – had been most insistent that Monty bought some live mice as well.

'Why?' asked the boy. 'To keep the snake company?'

'No,' said the pet shop owner. 'For lunch.'

For one horrible moment, Monty thought that the pet shop owner meant lunch for him, but of course he didn't.

The first scream from Mayflower was twice as loud as any that Monty had ever extracted. She was in her bedroom making glitter galoshes with her pet parrot, Polly, when the snake appeared over her shoulder, announced its arrival with a long hiss in her ear and tickled her cheek with its tongue.

'Oh my *AAAAAAAAAAAGH!!*' she screamed, shaking the pictures off the wall. 'Take it away. What is it?'

Monty stepped round from behind her. 'It's my new pet python,' he smiled, 'called SisterEater.' The name did its job and brought forth a second scream, which bounced around the bedroom like a rubber bullet and exploded in the light bulb. 'Its jaws are so huge,' continued Monty, 'it could fit all of you inside.'

'A … a … all of me?' stammered Mayflower.

'Yes, all of you!' roared Monty. 'Even your big feet and sticky-out pigtails. It could woofle you up like a single pea and still have room for pudding!'

Mayflower's brain could barely imagine a mouth so large and terrifying. It didn't have to. Monty got the snake to dislocate its lower jaw and show her.

'*AAAAAAAAAAAAAAAGH!*'

'What are you screaming at now?' Monty said innocently. 'I did tell you it had a big mouth so it can't be that.'

'No,' panted Mayflower, whose breaths were coming short and fast, 'a slimy green mouse just ran out of its mouth!'

She was not wrong. One of the live mice that Monty had bought from the pet shop had just sprinted across the snake's tongue, hopped over its teeth and run towards the skirting board.

'Oh yes,' said Monty casually. 'That was probably escaping from the snake's stomach. Snakes eat mice, you know.'

'But it was *alive*,' squeaked Mayflower.

'Of course it was! Don't you know anything about snakes? They only like to eat things if they're wiggling!'

'Wiggling!' she gasped.

'Wiggling,' he smirked. 'And you're the biggest wiggler I know!'

'AAAAAAAAAAAAAAAAAGH!'

Monty was going to have endless hours of fun with his sister!

* * *

He woke her the next morning with a breakfast tray.

'Wakey wakey!' he cried, drawing her bedroom curtains to let in the sun. 'I've brought you a mice cup of tea in bed!'

Mayflower yawned and rubbed her eyes. 'Thank you,' she said. 'Oh look, you've left the tea bag in the mug.' But when she grabbed the string to pull it out, it wasn't a string at all. It was a dead mouse's tail.

'AAAAAAAAAAAAAAAAGH!

'It was an accident,' Monty explained a few moments later, when his sister crept into the kitchen for a proper breakfast. 'I don't know what possessed that mouse to climb into your mug of tea. Maybe it was just thirsty.'

'Are you telling me the truth?' whispered Mayflower.

'Of course I am,' he replied. 'You're my sister. I love you.' And he was so convincing that she believed him. 'I really am sorry if I've upset you,' he continued. 'Will you let me make it up to you?'

'All right,' she smiled, feeling safe at last.

'Then sit down,' he said, tucking a napkin into the neck of her T-shirt. 'I've made you breakfast.'

'What is it?' she asked, as Monty placed an egg cup in front of her containing a round brown egg.

'It's a boiled mouse,' he said, flicking the lifeless tail and stiff little legs to make them wobble.

'*AAAAAAAAAAAAAAAAGH!*'

Later that evening, he pursued her into the bathroom, where it was Mayflower's habit to take a bath with the shower curtain drawn. This was perfect for Monty's purposes. He sneaked into the room undetected and with a cry of, 'Look out, there's a mouse in the house!' threw a live mouse over the top of the shower curtain. When it landed in Mayflower's bath water and started swimming, all hell broke loose.

'*AAAAAAAAAAAAAAAGH!*'

But Monty hadn't finished yet. While Mayflower flapped and yelled he pretended to come to her rescue. 'Never fear, SisterEater's here!' he proclaimed, sliding the snake into the water. 'He'll get rid of

that mouse for you!'

You'd have thought a bomb had exploded! While poor, screaming Mayflower dragged the curtain off its pole and flapped around in the water like a petrified pig in a crocodile pool, Monty left the bathroom with a sly grin and a casual quip over his shoulder. 'Have a mice day now!'

After a week, however, things began to go wrong for Monty. Because he was feeding his python so many mice the snake had grown and now that it was bigger, little mice no longer satisfied its massive hunger. The python pinned Monty up against his bedroom wall, while its stomach grumbled like a drain, and demanded something bigger.

'You don't mean me, do you?' said the boy nervously. 'Because I *am* your master, and traditionally pets are not allowed to eat their masters.'

The snake did *not* mean him, so Monty introduced the python to his sister's pet parrot.

'Polly, SisterEater. SisterEater, Polly,' he said,

opening Polly's cage so that the two pets could shake hands. Only SisterEater didn't have a hand to shake. When Mayflower trotted into the bedroom a few moments later, her precious parrot was nowhere to be seen. Actually, that's not quite true. She could see its shape bulging halfway down the snake's neck and hear its muffled voice, 'Who's a tasty boy, then?'

Needless to say, she screamed.

'AAAAAAAAAAAAAAAAGH!

Unfortunately, Monty was now caught in a vicious circle. Eating the parrot had made the snake grow again, which meant that Monty now had to find something even larger to feed it on. His eyes settled on his sister's cat, snuggled warmly in front of the fire.

When Mayflower came skipping into the sitting room with a ball of wool in her hand and called out, 'Cuddles. Oh Cuddles. It's playtime, Cuddles!' she saw something she never thought she'd see. 'Why is SisterEater curled up in front of the fire?' she asked uneasily.

'He's tired,' smiled Monty. 'He's just eaten.'

'So where's my pussy cat, Cuddles?' she cried.

'You haven't—?'

'I have!' sniggered her brother, kicking SisterEater awake. The python sat up showing off the lump of cat in its throat.

'Miaow,' came the muffled voice of Cuddles.

'*AAAAAAAAAAAAAAAAAGH!*'

came the clarion voice of Mayflower. Then she dropped the ball of wool and fled the room.

After the cat, it was Mayflower's pet lamb, Dimples. The python ambushed it while it was gambolling through the buttercup meadow and gobbled it up in one bite.

'*AAAAAAAAAAAAAAAAAGH!*'

> I'm going to treat you to one of my songs.
> Baa baa, black sheep
> Have you any head?
> No, sir, no, sir
> I think I'm dead.

After the lamb it was a small horse. Well, Mayflower's pony to be exact. Mayflower and her best friend, Miranda, had been riding it in the paddock when Miranda disappeared.

'Oh Monty!' cried Mayflower. 'Have *you* seen Miranda?'

'I don't think I have,' said Monty. 'No, wait a moment. What's that?' He pointed into the paddock where a large python, its stomach distended with the bulk of a pony and rider, was jumping a five-bar gate. 'Is that her in the saddle?'

'*AAAAAAAAAAAAAAAAAGH!*'

And after the pony? A cow. And after the cow? A coachload of tourists visiting the farm shop. And after the coach load of tourists visiting the farm shop? Well, nothing!

Mayflower had run out of pets and the farm had run out of big animals. There was nothing left to feed to Monty's python. Monty did consider sacrificing his sister, but his mother put a stop to that. She took one look at her daughter marinating in a pot with a giant python drooling over the top of her, and threw herself across the table as a human shield.

'*Don't you dare!*' she yelled at Monty.

'You're quite right,' he said, leading his python

outside into the yard. 'There'd be no fun in it. If SisterEater ate my sister, who would watch and scream!' And that was the point. Monty only did these terrible things to upset his sister.

But it didn't work out quite as Monty planned!

HEEEEEEEEELP!

With no food, Monty had come to the end of the line.

There was only one thing he could do with his pet.

'You can't throw it away!' shrieked Mayflower. 'I thought you didn't like it,' said Monty, who had the snake's head in one dustbin, its tail in another and the coils of its body in six more.

'I *don't* like it,' said Mayflower. 'I hate it. But you can't put a pet in the bin just because it's too big.'

'Then I shan't,' said Monty. 'I shall flush it down the loo instead!'

He was at it for days, pushing every coil around the bend with the loo brush. In the end, it was too big to flush away entirely and too heavy to pull back up and start again. This meant, of course, that Monty had to leave it down the pan and couldn't go to the loo.

'Are you scared of being bitten?' giggled Mayflower.

'No,' he said, when he *was*. 'Are you?'

'Not at all,' said his sister, who had miraculously come out of her shell since saving the python from the dustbin. 'In fact, because I  saved his life, SisterEater and I are the best of friends now,' she said. 'He lets me go to the loo whenever I want. But you, on the other hand—' she burst into peals of laughter '—you'll just have to cross your legs for the rest of your whole life!'

'You're enjoying this, aren't you?' he said.

'Oh yes!' she cried. 'Because you'll *have* to go sometime, and when you do, SisterEater will burst out of the bowl and bite your winkle off! Ha ha ha!' And she didn't stop laughing all night.

I love this job. Take a timid girl like Mayflower. Not a bad bone in her body. The chances of her booking into The Darkness? Zero. Then one day she meets a python who brings out the brute in her and I'm rushed off my hooves getting her hothell room ready!

✸ ✸ ✸

On the fourth night of not using the loo, Mayflower's prediction came true. Monty could not keep his legs crossed any longer. Despite the obvious danger, he dashed into the smallest room in the house, where – as you might have guessed – the hacked-off demon of the deep was waiting to grab him. With a zip and a splash

51

and an almighty chomp, Monty disappeared around the bend with his head in the jaws of a python!

When Monty came round, he could hear running water. The air was dank and fetid. A taste not unlike bad eggs clung to the back of his throat. He opened his eyes slowly to find that he was perched on a narrow ledge with his feet dangling in a stream of thick, brown, slow-moving water. He was in the sewers.

Looking either side, he was astonished to see thousands of glum-faced children sitting on the ledge next to him. Around their necks, each of them was wearing a collar which had a small metal name-tag attached. The tags jangled softly like cow bells and echoed eerily off the curved brick walls.

'What's the matter with you lot?' Monty said, pointing down the long Victorian tunnel which narrowed to a tiny dot of light at the end. 'Down there. Look! There's a way out.' Nobody seemed that pleased. Instead, a small girl with pale white skin and dark rings around her eyes tapped him on the shoulder.

'You're not going anywhere,' she said, pointing across the sludgy stream at the wall opposite.

Monty looked up and gasped. Thousands of sparkling eyes stared back at him through the darkness. The wall was lined with watching animals: crocodiles, spiders, praying mantises, hamsters, mice, snapping turtles, crabs, rats, snakes and scorpions.

'This is *our* place,' they hissed menacingly. 'You're *our* pets now!'

Monty felt around his own neck and jumped with fright. He too was wearing a collar. 'Are those all your pets?' he asked the other children. 'The pets that you got bored with and flushed down the loo?'

'Yes,' trembled the pale-faced girl. 'They keep us here for their amusement, and when they don't want us anymore, they eat us!'

'Right, I'm off!' roared Monty, and he plunged off the ledge into the river of stink. 'You can't keep me here!' he screamed, as he swam towards the light.

'Oh yesss I can!' boomed a voice from the shadows. Suddenly, SisterEater dropped down in front of Monty and opened wide his jaws. His mouth was as big as the tunnel itself. 'You can run if you like,' said Monty's python, 'but I'm soooo hungry, I might just bite! Go on, Monty. Make my day!'

But Monty thought he wouldn't. On balance, he felt, it was better to stay put and do as he was told, like an obedient little pet.

He's still down there now; still fetching sticks; still hoping his master won't get bored and eat him. If you don't believe me, do what Mayflower does every night before bed. She puts her head down the pan and listens for her brother's cries. And when she hears him call out.

'Heeeeeeeeeeeeeeeeelp!'

she laughs '*Aagh-ha-ha-ha-a*,' a cold little laugh of revenge.

I must confess, it's very satisfying when bad children do my work for me. The Sewer Rats are already captives in a living hell, so that lets me out of having to house them here in The Darkness.

54

It saves me having to cough up for food and gives me more empty rooms for children like YOU! By the way when I say 'cough up for food'. I do mean what I say. Never knock a phlegm sandwich till you've tried one!

Excuse me a moment

That should shut him up for a while!

'HEEEEEELP!'

'I wan—!'

Not now.

Talking of food, have you ever heard a lobster scream? Cry out in pain as it's PLUNGED into boiling water by a chef? If you have you're the only person in the world, because lobsters don't scream. They die the second they touch the water. Greedy little girls, on the other hand, are quite a different kettle of cuttle. They make a terrible noise when they're boiled, which is probably why you've never seen **GIRL THERMIDOR** on menus in top restaurants.

You do in restaurants down here, though!

I've got a greedy little girl in Room 492.561. Her name is Shannon Shellfish and she's greedier than every other greedy girl put together. She's quite pretty in a sort of stampy, pouty-faced way, but she makes herself look extremely unattractive by tagging the words 'I want' onto the front of every sentence.

'I wan—!'   Nothing! Give it a rest!

What she wants to say is, 'I want to get out of here right now!' but I don't want her to. And down here, what I want goes!

56

THE LOBSTER'S SCREAM

It started when Shannon Shellfish was very young. In the maternity hospital, thirty seconds after she was born, she took one look at her exhausted, weeping, puffy-eyed mother and shouted, **'I want a more beautiful mummy!'**

Two days later, when her parents took her home and she stared up at the house from inside her pram, she yelled, **'I want a bigger house!'** And on her first birthday she threw all of her presents back at her parents with a cry of, **'I want a week in EuroDisney!'**

As you can probably guess, Shannon's mother did not swap herself for a less tired mummy and her father did not sell the house, but they *did* take all her presents back to the shops and pay for a week at EuroDisney instead.

It didn't matter to Shannon that the week

was a disaster. Being only a year old she slept most of the time, and when she finally did wake up she wasn't allowed on the rides anyway, because she failed the minimum height restriction. The point was that by going to EuroDisney Shannon had got her own way and as far as she was concerned that gave her the green light to try and get her own way again … and again … and again … and again.

From that moment onwards Shannon Shellfish shouted **'I want!'** a thousand times a day, and because she always got what she wanted, she started to believe that the words were magic!

This is how it went most days in the Shellfish family.

Imagine a perfect scene around the supper table. Shannon has shepherd's pie and sprouts on her plate. Mr Shellfish has shepherd's pie and  sprouts on his plate. Mrs Shellfish has shepherd's pie on her plate and is *adding* the sprouts – to be exact, they are in mid-air, on the serving spoon betwixt bowl and plate.

Now, not wanting her mother to have anything that she doesn't have, Shannon waits for the last sprout to roll on to her mother's plate before howling, 'I want that sprout!'

Naturally enough, Mrs Shellfish laughs at her daughter's ridiculous request and says, 'It's on my plate now, Shannon.'

This, however, does not put Shannon off. **'But I want it!'** she bawls, and goes on in a similar vein for five loud minutes until finally her father cracks.

'Just let her have it!' he cries. 'It's only a sprout!' So the sprout is lifted off the mother's plate and relocated to Shannon's, where it sits for a good ten minutes until Shannon makes an announcement.

'Ugh!' she says. 'It's cold. Don't want it now.'

This, in a nutshell, was the problem. Whatever Shannon wanted was always wasted. The truth was she didn't really want anything – except to be the boss and make her parents run around after her.

Time for another song . . .

Snip snap.
Clickety clack.
Bubble, trouble.
Hell and back!

You'll find out what it means in a minute.
Isn't it exciting! Just the thought of finding
out gets me frothing!

Birthdays always brought out the worst in
Shannon and her eleventh one was no
exception.

**'I want it! I want it! I want it! I
want it!'** They were passing a
pet shop at the time.

'Want what, dear?' said her
mother.

'A pet!' screamed Shannon.
'Something. I don't care.
Anything. Everything. That dog –
there.' She pointed to a puppy in a
basket. It had black rings around its eyes
like sunglasses.

60

'You want *that* dog?' Mr Shellfish sighed wearily.

'Yes. That dog for my birthday present. **I want it really badly!**' So they went inside.

Before they bought the puppy, however, Mr and Mrs Shellfish were extremely sensible and said all the right things. 'You will look after it, won't you?' her mother said and her father added, 'A dog is for life not just for your birthday.'

Shannon nodded in all the right places and convinced her parents and the pet shop owner that she was mature and responsible enough to look after another life. But when she got the dog home, it stained her favourite duvet brown and wiped its face on her flannel. So she chucked it in a skip.

Any normal parents would have handed in their child to the police or sent them on a long holiday to the salt mines of Siberia . . .

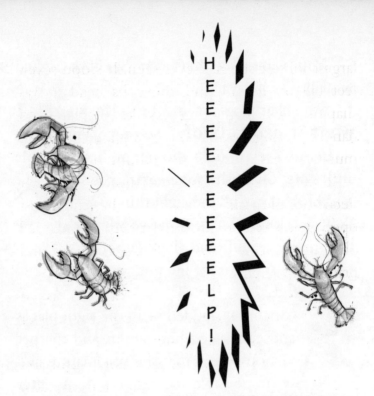

HEEEEEEELP!

... but not Mr and Mrs Shellfish. Numbnuts that they were, they asked Shannon what she'd like instead! For once, Shannon did not know. She sat at the kitchen table and pondered the wish list in her head. She had just narrowed it down to a pony or cash, when the fickle pincer of fate rang the doorbell.

When Shannon opened the door she got the shock of her life. Standing on the step was the largest lobster she had ever seen. It stood seven feet tall on its tail, and above its head it was snapping its huge pincers like a Flamenco dancer playing the maracas. It was a magnificent mutation that was, as it turned out, not real.

'Hubble, bubble, boil and trouble,' said Mr Pecorino, the Italian man inside the suit. 'I just open a new restaurant in the town.' He handed Shannon a printed leaflet. 'Please to come and bring your friends.'

'What's it called?' asked Shannon, eyeing the lobster suit closely.

'Hubble Bubble Boil and Trouble. I just tell you. We make very good lobsters.'

'That's what I want!' exploded Shannon so suddenly that the man in the lobster suit thought he had trodden on her toe.

'Sorry,' he said. 'I don't know how big my own tail is.'

'MUMMY!'

Shannon's mother came running. 'Yes, dear.'

'I know what I want for my birthday.'

'Can't it wait, dear? I'm icing your cake.'

'I want that lobster costume.' This was the first time Mrs Shellfish had noticed the seven-foot lobster standing outside her front door.

'Oh,' she said.

'Good afternoon,' said the lobster, extending a pincer of friendship. 'Mr Pecorino. Hubble Bubble Boil and Trouble. Please to come along and taste our lobsters.'

'Well?' interrupted Shannon. 'What are you waiting for, Mummy? Get the suit off him!'

Mrs Shellfish wasn't sure she should. 'The nice man probably needs it, dear.'

'But I WANT it!' howled her daughter.

Mr Pecorino had heard enough, besides he'd wasted too much time already. 'OK. I go now. Bye bye.'

But Shannon always got what she wanted. 'NOT SO FAST!' she yelled, diving full length across the front step to rugby tackle the lobster to the ground.

'Help!' cried Mr Pecorino, who lay stranded on his back like a beetle. 'What you do?'

'I want your lobster costume!' screamed Shannon.

Mr Pecorino had never been spoken to like this by a child before. 'Have no one ever told you, signorina . . .

'I WANT NEVER GETS!'

'Yes, it does,' said Shannon, grabbing something off the grass and sitting on the lobster's chest. 'Or I'll poke your eyes out with this sharp stick.'

'OK. OK. I listen!' Mr Pecorino was noted for his lobster, not his bravery. 'Here's the deal. You come to my restaurant tonight, eat my lobsters, pay my bill and you can have the suit. That way, *I* win and *you* win.'

'If you're lying,' hissed Shannon, leaning down and whispering in the lobster's ear, 'I'll find you. Only the stick I'll bring with me won't be sharp like this one. It'll be blunt. So more pain in the eyeballs. OK?'

'I not lie!' squealed Mr Pecorino, struggling to get away. There was a loud crack and he stopped dead. 'Owwww!' he cried. 'I think you break my tail.'

> Gurgle! Goo-goo!

> Who's there? Is that you, Garth? I thought I told you to stay in your room until you'd had your nappy changed

* * *

Shannon's parents pointed out to Shannon that in order to fulfil her side of the bargain she had to eat lobster.

'So?' she said.

'And you're happy with that?' asked her father.

'Why?'

'Because you don't like lobster,' said her mother.

'Not bothered,' said Shannon.

'Well, you should be,' said Mr Shellfish. 'You can't cook a lobster then *not* eat it.'

'Oh dear, how rude of me!' jeered Shannon all of a sudden. 'I didn't see the door open and the world expert on lobsters come into the room. In case you need reminding, Daddy, I can do anything I want.'

Her father lowered his voice to a growl. 'You obviously don't know why lobsters turn red when they're cooked,' he said.

'Are you trying to scare me?' mocked his daughter. 'Well, you're not succeeding, because I still want a lobster costume!'

'They turn red, because they're furious at being boiled alive,' he explained.

'They have terrible tempers,' cried Mrs Shellfish. 'When they're angry their pincers go snip, snip! Snip, snip, snip! Snip …'

But Shannon wasn't impressed. What harm could a teeny-tiny lobster do to *her*?

'You're not listening,' she said. Then she screamed until the veins in her forehead stood out like knotted string. 'It's my birthday and **I want a lobster costume.** OK?'

When her super-soft parents agreed to her demands, it was a huge relief to me, because if they hadn't she would never have ended up in the soup... lobster bisque, of course!

Now that she was going out to a posh restaurant for her birthday, Shannon had a whole new list of *wants*. First up, she wanted a new dress.

'But you already have hundreds of new dresses in your wardrobe,' gasped her mother. 'I bought you a new one every week last year and you never wear them.'

'I've never been this old before, have I?' said Shannon. 'Those dresses were bought for a younger girl. Besides, this is a special occasion and I want to wow the crowds outside the restaurant!'

'Crowds!' tittered her father. 'There won't be any crowds.'

'Then get me some!' came the order. 'For once in my life, **I want to feel special!'**

So her father contacted Rent-A-Crowd and organised a welcoming party while her mother took her to the shops to buy that dress. Only when they got there it wasn't just one dress . . .

'They're *all* so beautiful!' Shannon cried, snatching three off one rail and adding them to the pile of mohair in her mother's arms.

'**I want this!** And this! And this! And that! And these!' She jumped onto a mannequin's plinth and made a sweeping gesture across the boutique. '**I want everything I can see!**'

But when they got outside, Shannon went off the lot and dumped them in a skip. Right on top of a puppy, as it happened.

'Ugh!' she sneered. 'Wouldn't be seen dead in those!'

Her mother pursued her up the street and asked her what she would be seen dead in, but Shannon didn't know. 'We'll just have to go on until I find something I want,' she said.

I always recommend a shroud for being seen dead in. It's what every corpse is wearing this year!

Oink! Oink!

Apart from Truffle, obviously. He's wearing pig skin.

They tried on a mile of dresses, but none was quite right. As far as Shannon was concerned they were variously too long, too short, too black, too brown, too low, too high, too feathery, too frumpy, too flowing or too nice. It took her mother calling a dress 'Too much!' to bring Shannon to a decision.

'But I WANT this one!' she cried. 'It's my birthday! How can you put a price on your precious daughter's happiness?' It was inevitable that Shannon would want the most expensive. Mrs Shellfish handed over her credit card with a squirm of embarrassment.

'Charge it up,' she said.

✱ ✱ ✱

Now that the dress was sorted, the next thing Shannon wanted was a white limousine. At least she did until it was booked and then she wanted something else.

'I can't go to a swanky restaurant in a boring old limousine,' she said. **'I want to go in a helicopter.** And when I arrive I want the crowd to be cheering. I want someone to open my door, I want a red carpet, I want lights, I want fanfares, I want the crowd to the press lined

70

up with their cameras, and I want a choir of sweet little schoolboys singing *Hallelujah!*' She stared at her parents. 'What?!'

They stared back as if she'd taken leave of her senses.

'What's wrong?'

'Will there be anything else?' mocked Mr Shellfish. His daughter spat back like a snake.

'Don't be sarcastic, Daddy. It's not clever.' And Daddy being Daddy, Daddy did as he was told.

> I want Shannon to get everything she's ever wanted and not check in to The Hothell Darkness so I can tease the badness out of her! Oh dear. I just remembered. 'I want never gets!' What a pity. I'll just have to give her a room after all!

* * *

The night unfolded as expected. Shannon's parents knew that their daughter would reject everything she'd asked for, and sure enough she did.

Before they'd even left home she clumped down the stairs in her new long

71

evening gown and with a cry of **'I want it shorter!'**, tore a strip off the bottom until it was a miniskirt. She felt sick in the helicopter, so pulled off the pilot's headphones and bellowed, **'I want to walk!'** She grew tired of the rented crowds outside the restaurant and sent them packing with a shriek of **'I want to be alone!'** And in the restaurant itself, she ordered the largest lobster in the tank . . . and then refused to eat it.

'I don't *want* lobster!' she screamed when Mr Pecorino placed the plate down in front of her. Mr Shellfish thought he'd made himself clear on the question of not leaving lobster and firmly corrected his daughter's manners.

'I'm sorry, Shannon, but you've ordered it, you have to eat it.'

'Don't want to,' she sulked.

Mr Pecorino had stopped smiling. 'But it is cooked now!' he said firmly. 'You *must* eat it or the lobster he die for nothing.' Shannon pushed the plate away from her.

'I don't do what other people want me to do, Mr

Lobster-Man. I only do what I want to do, **and I want my present!** OK?!'

'I thought we have a deal,' growled Mr Pecorino. 'Eat first, costume later.'

'Then you thought wrong,' replied the girl, 'because I hate lobster! It makes me sick!'

'Oh dear,' trembled Mrs Shellfish, screwing the corners of her napkin into the cooked lobster's ears. 'I do hope it can't hear you.'

But of course it could. And the more the lobster heard, the crosser it became. Lobsters are very similar to human beings. They're not that keen on being boiled alive for no good reason.

Meanwhile, Shannon had left the table and chased Mr Pecorino into the kitchen, where she had picked up a wooden spoon and was once again threatening to poke his eyes out unless he gave her what she wanted. He showed her the cupboard where he kept the lobster costume and left her to climb into it.

In the restaurant, however, the unwanted cooked lobster had reached the end of its tether. Steam rose from its shell as it gestured angrily to its live friends in the tank by the window. It stood on its red tail and clicked its pincers above its head like an angry tic-tac man. The effect was instantaneous. The live lobsters formed a lobster ladder in the water and climbed over each other's backs until they could reach the lip of the tank. Then they threw themselves out onto the floor. Other diners stood up quickly and rushed into the street before the tide of pincers pinched them. The floor was heaving with black crustaceans, moving like an oil slick towards the kitchen door.

Just then Shannon emerged from the kitchen wearing the lobster costume.

'I want someone to zip me up!' she announced to the empty room. The lack of diners came as something of a shock.

'Shannon!' shouted Mrs Shellfish.

'Walk towards us now!' cried her father. 'And don't look down!'

But nobody *ever* told Shannon what to do!

The moment she looked down, however, she wished she hadn't. It was like looking into a bottomless black sea. The lobsters swarmed over her feet and up her legs and body. They knocked her onto her back and picked her up in their pincers.

'What are you doing?' she yelled. **'I want you to stop. I want to get down!'**

But too many years of being pushed around by humans have made lobsters immune to such pleadings. With cold, armour-plated fury they scuttled into the kitchen where a large pot of water was still on the boil. Then they passed her over their heads towards the bubbling.

'No!' she yelled. 'No! I don't want to go in there! No! It's hot! Eeeeyoooooooooooooow!'

And that was the first and last time that a lobster has ever screamed.

She's screamed quite a lot since, though!

HEEEEEEEEEEEEEEEEEEEEEEEELP!

Oh for goodness' sake! Does Monty never shut up?

Who's that shouting out now?
There's never a moment's peace in this hothell. I
love it because it means I'm doing something right!
Oh. I might have guessed. Room 492.572. The
Crybaby! He hasn't stopped complaining since his
soul showed up last month. There wasn't much of
him left apart from his soul. He had half a lip and
one thumb, as I recall, which he was still sucking.

NEXT-AN INTERESTING FACT

Because I know everything, I know that
you will be extremely happy when you move
in here.

> Don't listen to the nasty big man!
> Gurgle! Goo, goo! He's an ickle liar!

> Yup! That cat seems to have got his tongue!

His name is Garth MacQueen, a boy for whom the
term 'nasty little beast' might have been invented.
His story starts as far back as the seventeenth
century, when babies living in
the Scottish Highlands were
snatched by wild wolves and
devoured in the woods like
flightless chickens!

In 1743, the last of the wild
wolves was killed by a man
called Eagan MacQueen — notice

the same last name. It was
Eagan MacQueen who cut off
the beast's head and gave it to
his wife to put in the pot. But
as the stock boiled and the head
slowly rolled in the upsurge of
bubbles, the wild wolf's steel-grey eyes
swivelled in their sockets and drank in one
last look at their destroyer before clouding
over for good.

Eagan MacQueen had been eyeballed. The wild
wolf's revenge was astir. It would, however, be
THREE HUNDRED YEARS before it came to
completion.

It was well worth waiting for, though!

WOLF CHILD

Living on the edge of the Darnaway Forest were
the wolf slayer's descendants: Elspet and Callum
MacQueen, their son Garth, and newborn baby,
Moira. Their house was on a modern estate built
on top of the spot where Eagan MacQueen had
stewed the wolf's head.

The residents were nervous. There had been
unconfirmed sightings of wild wolves in the
forest, which the police had dismissed as
superstitious nonsense. Then a gillie had died
hunting stags and a grandmother picnicking
with her grandchildren had seen their roast
chicken taken off by a 'beast with steel-grey
eyes'. Such stories fuelled rumours that
the wild wolves had returned, and with
them came fear. The crash of a dustbin
lid or the squeak of an unlocked gate in
the middle of the night was enough to
make grown men sit up in their beds and
quiver.

'We must take great care with the new

baby,' said Callum at supper one night. Moira was only a week old and had just come home from the hospital. 'Never let her out of your sight, Elspet, for the wolves need only a moment to snatch her.'

'Is it true about the wild wolves coming back?' asked Garth. 'Are they living in the garden?'

Callum chuckled. 'Nay, son. There's nothing to bother yourself about. 'Tis only the wee babies they take.'

'You mean Moira?' Garth gasped with horror. 'They might take my baby sister?' Then quite suddenly, his look of concern burst into an evil grin. 'Cool,' he said. 'Bring them on!'

❋ ❋ ❋

Garth had a problem with his baby sister. He didn't like her. Ever since she'd arrived nobody had paid him any attention. When his mother had brought the baby home, Garth had greeted her at the front door. He had stood there with his arms outstretched for a kiss, but she hadn't seen him and had knocked him down with her knee. And now if he wanted her to read him a book at bedtime, he had to push Moira off his mother's lap while the baby was feeding. It was as if Garth had become invisible. Maybe, he thought, watching his mother and father fawning over Moira in the bath, if he behaved like a baby his parents would start noticing him again.

'Actually, that's not a bad idea,' he muttered to himself.

It wasn't a bad idea. It was a DREADFUL idea! But not in a way that Garth could ever have predicted

From that day on, Garth behaved like a baby. At lunchtime, he sucked his thumb on the bus and cried when his mother slapped the back of his hand.

'Oh cruel, Mummy! Waaaaaah!' he wailed in his baby voice. 'Why you no let baby sucky thumb?'

His mother looked at him askance. 'What sort of language is that for a ten year old?'

The language of control, thought Garth. It

wraps you round my little finger. He didn't say it out loud, obviously, in case she had a blue fit.

✽ ✽ ✽

Later, in the supermarket, he insisted on being carried and, when his mother said no, he stopped in the aisle, dug in his heels and refused to move until she did as she was told!

'Behave, Garth!' A mother does not take orders from her own son.

'But baby am tired, Mumsy-wumsy. Me wanna sit on your shoulder-woulders.'

'No!'

'Garthy am wanna sleepy-byes.'

'Stop talking like a baby.' When his mother raised her voice that meant she was losing her cool, and that meant it was time to turn the emotional screw. It was time for baby to howl!

'Waaaaaah!' he screeched. 'Mumsy-wumsy's cross with me! Waaaaaah!'

'Garth!' she hissed, as all eyes turned to stare. 'Stop that! Everyone's looking!'

When his mother hissed with embarrassment it was all over; game set and match to Garth.

'Carry me, then,' he gloated with

82

outstretched arms and a scheming smile.

At dinner that night he threw a tantrum. He hurled his plate at his parents and covered them with half-chewed carrots and potatoes.

'Baby don't like vegetables!' he screamed. 'It's pooh!'

And at three o'clock in the morning, with a light drizzle falling outside, he woke his parents up by climbing into their bed with a pillowcase full of toys.

'Me and my toys is scared of the tunder and lighting!' he lied, emptying the contents of the pillowcase on top of his parents' heads. 'Oh, Mumsy-wumsy, what's wrong? Why is yous crying?'

'You've just dropped a car on the bridge of her nose!' fumed Mr MacQueen. 'Now act your age, Garth, and go back to bed!' But this only had one effect.

'Dadda's shouting at baby! Waaaaaah!'

✹ ✹ ✹

The next day he strawberry jammed the kitchen wallpaper, painting a gruesome picture

83

of wild wolves gobbling up a little girl. He showed it to Moira and grinned with cruel delight.

'That's not jam coming from the ickle sister's head!' he said. 'That's blood! And that ickle sister's *you*!' His tone was so viperous that her bottom lip began to wobble. 'And there's blood all over, because you is DEAD!' Moira burst into tears and didn't stop for two days.

Then, on Thursday, he was sick in the car. Not once but twice, and both without warning.

'Oops! Sorry, Dadda.'

'Why didn't you tell me you felt unwell?' protested his father who had got every last drop of stomach-soup down his neck.

'I'm a baby,' said Garth. 'I don't know how to stop myself.'

His father slammed on the brakes and got out to clean himself up. 'I don't know what's got into you, Garth.'

'I think what got into me was all this chocolate what I ate,' he grinned, showing his father the empty wrapper off a half-kilo bar of Dairy Delight.

'I don't mean that,' snapped his father. 'I mean all this baby stuff. If you don't grow up quick, son, the baby-bolting wolves will be coming for *you*!'

'Ooh, I am scared,' mocked Garth. 'Double up my nappy!'

But he should have been scared for the forest had ears. As they drove on along the road that bisected Darnaway Forest, a pair of steel-grey eyes swivelled in their sockets and followed the path of the car. A grey tail twitched in the undergrowth and a rough, pink tongue scraped along slavering lips.

I'll let you into a secret. It wasn't me!

It was Garth MacQueen's turn to be eyeballed.

* ** *

That night, Garth had a terrible dream. In his dream he was asleep in bed, when a knock at the door awakened him. Confident that it could only be his parents outside, he wound them up by crying out like a baby.

'Mamma, Dadda! Me is so scared of the big

bad wolf. Baby Garfy want a cuddle! Mamma, Dadda! Come and save your baby Garfy!'

The door handle turned slowly, leading Garth to believe that his parents were doing as they were told and coming in to save him. He cried out to encourage them. 'Goo-goo. Gaga. Goo-g . . .'

But the childish noises stuck in his throat when, instead of his parents, four wild wolves slunk through the door.

'No, no!' he yelled. 'I'm not a baby really. I'm ten years old. I'm nearly a man. I only did it to get attention from my Mummy and Daddy, but I'll stop now. I will. Please! If you're hungry you can take my sister instead. She's a *real* baby. No. She is! No. Go away!'

But the wild wolves weren't going anywhere without their prize. They stopped by the side of the bed, picked their teeth with their razor-sharp claws, leered like a gang of cut-throats and pounced. Garth struggled, but could not escape their crushing jaws. He felt their hard teeth sink through his flesh and bruise his bones; he smelled their rank breath; he stared deep into their cold, grey eyes and saw himself reflected there, floppy and limp like a lifeless baby.

Then he woke up, screaming. As he sat up in the dark and panted with fear, Garth vowed never to behave like a baby again. What if the wild wolves came while he was *pretending* to be a baby? Instead of Moira, they might snatch *him*! He was ten years old and from now on he *was* going to act his age; every day of every week of every month of every year! He was giving up baby for good!

Unfortunately, it was an ickle bit late for that!

Outside the window, a metal dustbin rolled noisily across the mud and banged against a wire fence. In front of a hole in this fence a freshly-made paw print glistened in the moonlight, and above it, snagged on the bent barbed wire, was a warm clump of grey fur. Garth saw none of these, nor noticed the tiny puncture mark on his arm still wet with wolf spit. Maybe his dream had not been a dream after all.

* * *

Early the next morning, when Garth swung his legs over the side of the mattress to get out of bed, he received a nasty surprise. His feet didn't touch the floor. In fact, his feet were rushing up to meet him. His legs were getting shorter! He knocked the side of his head with the heel of his hand to wake himself up, but he wasn't asleep. He jumped down off his bed and his feet landed in his slippers which were six sizes too big.

'What's going on?' he puzzled, as he ran across the wide open space that now separated the bed from the basin. The space had grown. And when he arrived at the basin to brush his teeth he was too small to see over the rim. This was no joke. Garth threw a skipping rope over the back of a chair and pulled himself up onto the seat. If he stood on his tiptoes he could just see the top of his head in the mirror. There was no doubt about it. He was shrinking!

No joking this time. Garth needed his mummy and daddy NOW!

'Help!' he screamed. 'Help! Mummy! Daddy! Save me!' But his words bubbled out as a string of gurgle and spit.

He rolled off the chair and hit the floor hard. No matter. He would reach the door, open it, let himself out and find his parents. But he couldn't stand up. He couldn't walk. His legs weren't strong enough. So he *crawled* to the door, stumbling twice on his weak elbows, but when he stretched up for the handle, it was out of his reach. 'Mummy! Daddy!'

In their bedroom, Garth's parents only heard a baby's cry. 'Gurgle! Goo-goo!'

'Is that Garth?' sighed Mrs MacQueen, rubbing her eyes and shaking herself awake.

'Ignore the selfish boy,' said her husband. 'He's just seeking attention again.'

Which was why Garth's parents ignored him all the next day, when he lay on his back in his bedroom and screamed and screamed, and wet his trousers. He only stopped screaming when his mother stuck a dummy in his mouth.

Gurgle! Goo-g—

But the day after that, when Garth's teeth and hair fell out during tea, his parents started to worry.

'You're not acting any more, are you?' said Mr MacQueen fearfully.

'Gurgle! Goo-goo!' replied Garth.

'Something happened that night to change you.'

'Gurgle! Goo-goo!'

'Oh, Callum, no!' cried Garth's mother. 'Don't you see... the shrinking, the talking, the toothless gums! It's wolf-witchery. He really *has* turned into a baby!'

The descendants of Eagan MacQueen heard a lupine howl outside and both blanched.

'*Moira!*' Elspet had left their other baby in the pram in the garden! 'I put her outside for some fresh air!'

Mr and Mrs MacQueen rushed out of the house, leaving Garth alone in the front room, lying on a blanket, chewing on a rusk. They stumbled into the garden, expecting to find their beautiful baby girl flopped in the jaws of a child-chomping wolf, but the pram was exactly where Elspet had left it. Moira was safe. Then, at exactly the same moment Elspet and Callum had exactly the same thought.

'Garth!' she gasped, her face etched with terror. 'They've got in behind us!'

'What have we done?' he howled. 'I told him not to behave like a baby. What did I say? If he didn't grow up quick, the wolves would come for *him*! But he wouldn't listen. HE WOULDN'T LISTEN!'

They rushed back into the front room, but the wild wolves had outsmarted them. In the twinkling of a steel-grey eye, they had exacted their three-hundred-year revenge. Wild wolves are cunning creatures who hunt in packs. While one wolf howled a distraction in the back garden, tearing the parents away from their baby son, another slipped in through the open front window and snatched baby Garth by the nape of his neck.

And that was that. Nobody has seen Garth since. It is thought that the wild wolves took him into Darnaway Forest, but what happened after that is a mystery.

I don't think it is, really. Wolf-baby. Baby-wolf. Think about it. There's not much doubt in my mind. They don't share a common love of sport or cinema, do they? They can't discuss politics or go to the pub for a pint and a sandwich. No, I think we all know what happened. The wolves ate him. And jolly tasty he probably was too. Nice and plump.

Gurgle! Goo-goo!

Oh! They had him with mustard, apparently.

The best baby recipe I know is Hawaiian Baby, which is ridiculously simple. All you need is a barbecue, a grass skirt and a tin of pineapple chunks. And a baby, of course.

Ooh, I tell you what I've never tried and might be nice: baby burgers. There was a time when the bat in Room 493.111 would have liked those.

THE FRUIT BAT

Once upon a Turkey Twizzler, there lived a girl called Cherie Stone, which was an odd name for a girl who hated fruit. Instead of eating food that was good for her, she stuffed her face with sugary sweets and saturated fats: burgers, pizzas, chocolate, chips and fizzy pop. It did terrible things to her body. It blocked up her insides like a double dose of cement and meant that for the best part of a year she couldn't go to the loo. With nothing getting out, but plenty going in, she grew and grew and grew and grew until she was too big to fit in the smallest room in the house (not that she ever needed to go in there) and looked like a giant potato.

What did you just say? Yes you! WHAT IS A POTATO? You are pulling my tail, aren't you?

You don't know what a potato looks like?

'Hello thickos! Anybody home?'

If you're that ignorant maybe I don't want you down here. Actually, no. Cancel that. I can always find a use for you in the Bloodletting Room as a bit of old rag to mop up with!

Next - an interesting fact

NEXT AN INTERESTING FACT

For those of you who know nothing, the potato was brought back from South America by Sir Walter Raleigh in 1588. That means, peasants in William Shakespeare's day knew what a potato looked like. Even goats can describe a potato — at least they could if they could speak. A potato is sort of round and dirty with eyes where the weevils have burrowed.

Cherie Stone looked like a potato, because her bowels were bunged up. To get things moving, Mr and Mrs Stone took their daughter to the doctor, a shrew-faced Scottish man with a strong Glaswegian accent and bright red hair. He measured Cherie's girth and weighed her in a horse's harness before delivering his diagnosis.

'At's constipation,' he said gravely. 'Forty-thud case thus wick.'

'But what can we do?' asked Mrs Stone. 'She's so heavy I couldn't bring her on the bus.'

The doctor sat back in his chair and thought deeply. Finally, he leaned forward and offered his prescription. 'If ya wunt to poosh it oot, thar's noot as good as froot!'

So fruit it was.

Hang on. I'm twitching again. You do know what fruit is, don't you? OH COME ON! You must have seen it soft, sweet and squidgy; livens up a smoothie; tops off an ice cream? So you have seen it. Good.

But do you eat it? If you do, CURSES! You will lead a long and happy life. If you don't you'll be coming down here to live with me. So please, DON'T START EATING FRUIT NOW. And when you're NOT eating fruit promise me that you'll open your bedroom window and shout out;

'I DON'T EAT FRUIT' because then THEY will hear you! Hanging upside down off a branch, their ears will twitch and they'll hear you scream that there's fruit in your house that is NOT being eaten! And once they know that, you are doomed! And once you are doomed you are MINE! Because they will come, in the middle of the night. You will wake to the sound of snapping teeth and a long flicky tongue sucking all the juice out! And that's what I want. So don't eat fruit. Don't even look at it. Be bad. Be mine.

Oink! Oink!

Alternatively, be bacon stuffing.

Anyway, we'll save that for later. For the time being, let's get back to that stupid doctor (I hate doctors always interfering and making children BETTER!) telling Cherie to save her life by eating more fruit.

After the visit to the doctor, Mr and Mrs Stone went fruit the

96

loop. They dressed up in large gooseberry cotumes and threatened to kiss their daughter outside her school gates if she didn't eat fruit. So embarrassed was Cherie at the sight of her parents puckering in green tights that she changed schools and didn't tell them. Her parents stood outside her old school for a week until the police arrested them and confiscated their costumes.

At home, they hid fruit around the house, in every nook and cranny, so that it was always available to tempt their bulging daughter into a fruity nibble. They draped grapes over the shower head in the bathroom to lure her during her ablutions; they filled her wardrobe with oranges and grapefruit to bombard her when she opened the doors; they decorated the apples and pears with apples and pears; they replaced the furry dice on the rear view mirror of the car with furry kiwi fruit; they swapped door handles for bananas, the TV remote control for a slice of melon, and the dog for a pineapple on a lead, which caused untold problems when Cherie walked it past a greengrocer's and the pineapple got into a fight with a pawpaw. Yet despite her parents' ingenuity and invention, Cherie's interest in fruit remained fixed at zero.

✻ ✻ ✻

So Mr and Mrs Stone came up with a cunning plan. Reasoning that it was Cherie's *daytime* brain that vetoed the fruit, they decided to use her *sleeptime* brain to change her mind. They secretly sewed miniature speakers into her pillows, and when she went to sleep at night they played her tapes of the sound of luscious loganberries growing in the Scottish Lowlands, and succulent strawberries blossoming in Shard. Their idea was to reshape her dreams in a fruit-ward direction so that when she woke up the only thing she thought about was fruit!

And it worked – nearly.

Her brain created fruity landscapes in her dreams: a bright yellow lemon shone over coconut hills, while a banana punt floated down an orange juice river full of peachy fish and plum frogs. But no sooner had this fruit appeared in her dreams than the anti-fruit side of Cherie's brain invented squadrons of giant wasps that ate all the fruit and put a stop to the brainwashing.

Cherie Stone hated fruit and *nothing* was ever going to get her to eat it.

That's NOTHING as in SOMETHING that goes squeak! squeak! splat!

She still had the problem of getting her parents off her back, however. If only she could convince them that eating fruit was dangerous, maybe they would stop begging her to eat it.

It took her several days of brain-wracking to come up with a story, but when she did it was a corker.

'You see,' she said at breakfast, 'I would eat fruit, but I can't.'

'You mean you won't,' sulked her mother.

'No, *can't*.' Cherie grinned slyly. She rearranged her features to look terrified. 'Because of the fruit bats!'

'What have fruit bats got to do with anything?' said Mrs Stone.

'Because fruit bats are attracted by the smell of fruit,' replied Cherie.

'I know that,' said her mother. 'So what's your point?'

'My point is that if a girl eats fruit, the smell of fruit in her stomach attracts the fruit bats who love fruit beyond all measure. And they come in the middle of the night, screeching out of a darkling sky to devour her. And she dies horribly in her bed, screaming while the bats eat her, chomping through her flesh to get at the fruit inside. And in the morning, parents generally come in and find the bits that are left strewn out across the bed clothes, which is really horrible too and makes the parents scream. And *then* a stalk grows out of the girl's remains – out of her head if she's still got one – and keeps on growing while she's buried in her coffin!'

'I didn't know that,' said her mother, clearly not believing a word.

'It's true,' persisted Cherie. 'I read it in a kids' magazine called *Dead Fruit Eaters' Weekly*, which has got stories about all the millions of children who die from fruit related deaths every week!'

Her mother gasped and feigned concern. 'You're not going to die are you?' she said.

'I might do,' said Cherie, lowering her eyes to look pathetic, 'if you make me eat fruit.'

'Oh well,' said her mother, dropping all pretence at distress, 'at least you'll die healthy.' And she tossed a grape across the table for Cherie to catch.

'You don't believe me, do you?' said Cherie indignantly, as the grape bounced off her shoulder and fell to the floor.

'No. I've never heard such tummy rot in all my life! Fruit bats don't eat children.'

'Yeah well, they *do* actually,' shrieked Cherie, getting up from the table. 'So you can carry on buying fruit as much as you like, but it'll just go to rot, because I won't eat fruit. Never! Do you hear me?' Then she flounced out of the kitchen, slapping her father's newspaper on the way. When she reached the doorway she turned her vast bulk around to have the last word. 'You'll be sorry when I'm dead!' she bawled, and then she was gone, squeezing through the door and slamming it behind her.

'Not sure I will,' said Mr Stone.

I'm sure I won't!

What Cherie didn't know was that fruit bats have incredibly sensitive hearing. Nearby in the branches of a codling tree, when Cherie spoke the words 'So you can carry on buying fruit as much as you like, but it'll just go to rot, because I won't eat fruit. Never!' a pair of pointed ears stood rigidly to attention. Cherie was right about something; Fruit bats live for fruit. They love it more than life itself. So when this particular Fruit bat heard that fruit was going to waste, it had no choice but to find the fruit and eat it first. And that meant setting a course for Cherie Stone.

✳ ✳ ✳

Half an hour later, Cherie Stone was walking to school when she found a banana in her rucksack. Her mother had hidden it under her gym kit just in case her daughter suddenly felt peckish after netball. As Cherie tossed it into a bin the sound of a twig snapping close by made her freeze. She sneaked a glance over her shoulder to see if she was being followed.

'Hello,' she called out. 'Hello. Who's there?' Nobody replied.

Later, in the school dining hall, when Cherie opened her packed lunch box she found a peach. Her mother had lovingly sliced it and sneaked it in under her marshmallow sandwich. As she took the peach out to leave it on her plate, she heard a scuffling in the roof beams above her. She looked up, but there was nothing there.

And later still, on her way home from school, when she found a stupid kumquat in her pocket ... there it was again! That feeling that she was being watched. That something was out there, waiting to pounce. She threw the kumquat away and broke into a slow trot, to get home as quickly as she could.

Had she turned around Cherie would have seen a shadow with long, thin grasshopper legs scuttle out from behind a bush. She would also have seen a brown beast on the wing streak through the air and land with a squelch on the kumquat. It plunged its sharp teeth into the heart of the fruit and tore out the flesh like a jackal!

For supper Cherie Stone's mother had cooked upside-down pudding with raspberries on top, but Cherie stared out of the window and ate crisps instead.

'Did anyone else just see a shadow out there?' she asked nervously.

'If you're still trying to make me believe your silly fruit bat story, Cherie, forget it! Fruit bats do *not* eat little girls. There is *not* one in the garden. I do *not* believe you!' Her mother had lost her temper. 'You'll say anything to get out of eating fruit. Now, start your pudding.'

'No,' said her hulking daughter, leaving the room with a chocolate bar in her hand. 'Not hungry.'

And so to bed. To the reinforced bed custom-built by a bridge engineer to support Cherie's vast weight. She eased herself under the duvet and ate the bar of chocolate. Then she turned off the light, rolled onto her back and closed her eyes.

And so to sleep. *for the very last time!*

On her way to bed, Cherie's mother did what she did every night. She placed a tangerine on Cherie's pillow, in case her daughter should be woken by the ache of an empty stomach. But on this particular night, for no particular reason, she hesitated by the side of the bed and as a little afterthought, popped a plum in the pocket of Cherie's pyjamas – just above her daughter's pumping heart! Then she left the room and went to bed herself.

* * *

By midnight, Cherie was asleep. This meant that she didn't hear the noise at the window; the noise that sounded like the flapping of a shroud. The fruit bat landed on the ledge outside, pulled open the window with its claw, sniffed the air for fruit and stepped inside. It dropped to the floor with a thump, lurched across the wooden floorboards on its knuckles, hopped onto the bed and drew its wrinkled face level with Cherie's. It only wanted to eat the tangerine and then it would go. But once the tangerine had been devoured, its sensitive nose picked up another scent. The smell of something even sweeter and juicier; the smell of a real treat – the plum in Cherie Stone's pocket!

With mouth agape and gnashers glinting, the fruit bat lunged to take the plum, but the pocket was made from thick flannelette which muddled the fruit bat's radar. It lost its bearings and lunged too fast and too far, biting not only through the plum's skin, but through into Cherie's heart as well! Cherie opened her eyes and screamed as a spurt of bright-red blood hit the ceiling above her head. And then it was over. The blackness descended as the Fruit bat retired through the window and flew back to its codling tree having gorged on the fruit; flesh, juice, *stone* and all!

✻ ✻ ✻

When Cherie Stone woke up she didn't know where she was and wondered why she wasn't in bed any more. Her head felt like it was going to

burst, as if it was full of
blood and still filling. Her
feet felt strange too. The
muscles ached from gripping.
She heard voices below her and opened her eyes
to find that she was hanging off a branch. The
world was upside down.

'Look, it's woken up!' came the cry. She
peered down and saw three children standing
below her. She noticed too that she was holding
a codling apple in her hand and her mouth had
filled with water. There was nothing in the
world she wanted *more*. She took a bite and
licked her lips. It was delicious!

'Kill it!' shouted the little boy, hurling a stone
at Cherie's head. 'Knock it out the tree.'

The stone hit her on the gripping leg
and dislodged her claw. 'Help!' she cried
as she plunged towards the ground, but
her body knew what it was doing. As
her wings unfurled she pulled out of
the dive and Cherie realised what had
happened. An accidental bite to the heart
had turned her into a Fruit bat! Unfortunately
there was no time to dwell on her misfortune,
because the children were still throwing rocks at

her. She was still not out of danger. If they hit her and brought her down, they would stamp on her tiny head and burst her brains to billio! What could she do?

Luckily, that was when her tummy rumbled. *That* was when an unfamiliar gurgle bubbled in her gut and burst out behind her like an exploding slurry pit, shooting her into the sky with the force of a jet engine and showering her attackers in a noxious waterfall of stinking brown bat poo!

'Well, that was a bonus,' grinned the new slimmed–down bat-girl. After all, it had been the best part of a year since she'd been to the loo. Now, after eating just one codling apple, it was all systems go again. Then she turned due west and flew half way round the world into The Darkness.

I have my fun with her down here. Mainly at YOUR expense. I let her out sometimes to find some fruit. because it amuses me to think of someone like you underneath her when she eats a codling apple!

You do see what I mean. don't you?

Here's a word of warning: When Cherie's out and about don't leave home without an umbrella!

I should have known you wouldn't understand. If you don't know what a potato looks like how could I ever expect you to imagine a world where pedestrians are splattered in bat poo?

'HEEEEEEEEEEEEEEEEELP!'

Oh not again. I thought he'd gone away. I wish that python would do us all a favour and just eat him!

If that doesn't shut him up I don't know what will.

'Oy! Was that bat poo just went up my nose?'

'Might have been.' Haha! I love bats!

That's it. We've reached the end of our little journey through the Animal Wing. It will soon be time for you to wave goodbye to your old life and register with me. I hope these NASTY LITTLE BEASTS have taught you lots of new ways to be bad, because if they have it makes my job worthwhile.

There's one last story. It belongs to the child in Room 492.575. You can't miss it; it's the room that's been sealed with polythene to keep the smell in. The room is so filthy I've seen cockroaches packing their bags and leaving. It won't come as any surprise to you to know that the child inside is a BOY and his story is all about pigs . . .

What? What? WHAT?

No! Don't tell me you don't know what a pig looks like! A bit like a SAUSAGE only bigger, pinker, four more legs and bags more get up and go!

THE
CLOTHES
PIGS

This tale starts with a toasty-warm sunrise and a golden-fingered glow that creeps over the treetops and spills down the hill towards Cherry Tree Farm. It also starts with a full-throated cock crow and a rustling of sweet-smelling hay, with Gertude the duck and her fluffy little ducklings waddling across the farmyard, and with Daisy the cow nudging the stragglers to help them keep up. This tale starts with all the pretty animals on the pretty farm waking from a night of pretty dreams. There was Billy the goat, Roger the horse and Insy, Winsy, Nibble and Titch, the four little pink piglets. They were the smallest, sweetest, silliest little pink piglets

you ever did see and they were always getting into scrapes.

One day, for example, a solid sow called Bertha, who had taken up ballet to keep fit, was concentrating hard on getting her leg up onto the practice bar when the four little piglets tumbled into the sty playing catch tag. She didn't see them and accidentally trod on Insy. So startled was she by his squeal of pain that she lost her balance and crashed to the ground in a cloud of dust and giggles!

'Oh dear,' she cried, wiping tears of laughter from her eyes, 'I've seen ballet pumps bigger than you!'

It was true. When they were born Insy, Winsy, Nibble and Titch were no bigger than coffee beans, and because they never got any food they had barely grown at all. Their elder brothers and sisters had a way of reaching the slops first: shoulder barging, tail pulling, ear biting and kicking each other out of the way, to name but four. If you've ever seen pigs feeding at the trough you'll know exactly what I mean. It's a brutal business; noisy, ferociously blood-spattered and not a good manner in sight.

But enough of the nasties. The point is that deprived of food Insy, Winsy, Nibble and Titch were permanently hungry, and hungry pigs have got to eat sometime. It's just a question of *when*, *how* and *who*.

Close by to Cherry Tree Farm, in a big, smoky city unused to seeing pigs on the streets, there lived a misguided boy by the name of Truman Snuffle, or Truffle for short. Truffle was a slob of a child, who treated his home like a hotel and his parents like slaves. He made his father do all the heavy tasks around the house, such as carrying him up and down stairs, switching off his bedroom light or opening the toothpaste tube, while his mother did everything else. He never offered to clear up after she'd cooked him a meal. He never ran his own bath, or washed his own toes or made his own bed. He never changed his own channels on the telly, or turned his own keys in the front door, or put his own rubbish in the wastepaper bin. And he never (repeat *never*) picked up his own clothes. Clothes that his mother had spent hours washing, ironing, folding and putting away neatly in his cupboard, clothes that he chucked on the floor like a pig!

> Appropriate that, a pig . . .

Truffle's bedroom looked like a pigsty. Actually, it wasn't *just* his bedroom. Piles of discarded clothes were dotted around the house like steaming heaps of elephant dung dotted around a grassy plain: outside the bathroom, by the back door, in the hall, on the stairs, down the back of the sofa; little surprises for Truffle's mother to find and deal with - sweaty socks, crumpled T-shirts, and old pants. Never a day passed when Truffle's parents did not beg him to pick up his clothes and never a day passed when Truffle did not reply, 'I'd like to *pick up* a new set of parents!'

'This can't go on!' wailed his mother. They were standing in his pit of a bedroom. 'You're wearing me out. I finish clearing up one mess only to find you making another!'

'You're my *mother*,' said Truffle imperiously. 'It is your *job* to clear up around me. That is why you have been put here on this earth, and the sooner you get used to it the easier it will be for both of us.'

'Steady on,' said Truffle's father, but Mrs Snuffle did not need his support, she had a game plan all of her own.

'If you continue to turn my house into a pigsty,' she bristled, 'the Clothes Pigs will pay you a visit.'

'The *what*?'

'The Clothes Pigs.' She unhooked a grey sock from the lampshade and lifted a shoe off the bedside table. 'They're little piggies who live in pig sties like this! They'll get rid of you and that will be that!' Truffle poured scorn on his mother's pathetic attempt to frighten him.

'I'm not scared of little piggies!' he said.

'Well, you should be. They'll trotter you away.'

'Trotter me away!'

'Trotters, snouts, teeth! They use anything to get rid of you.'

'What they lack in size they make up for in cunning,' chipped in Mr Snuffle. 'But do as your poor mother says, Truffle - pick up your clothes - and you won't hear a squeal out of them.'

Unfortunately, Truffle now had the bit between his teeth. He was convinced that the Clothes Pigs were just a story that his parents had made up to correct his behaviour.

'I don't believe you,' he said boldly. 'I mean, for a start, I live in a city, and pigs are country animals. How are these Clothes Pigs going to get to me? Are they going to walk through the middle of a busy city in broad daylight? Do they know how to use a pelican crossing? Are they going to saunter past every Butchers Shop without being chased with a carving knife? I don't think so, do you?' This merely confirmed how pig-ignorant Truffle *was*. That is to say, how ignorant he was of the power of pigs!

Especially the LITTLE ones!

✱ ✱ ✱

Then the accident happened and Truffle's life went apple-sauce shaped.

His mother was carrying a pile of his washing across the landing when she tripped on a pant-hill that he'd left at the top of the stairs. She didn't stand a chance. She fell forward, only to find that the ground had disappeared from underneath her, and flew through the air until the stairs broke her fall. Sadly, they also broke her leg. She bumped down the last three steps and crumpled into a heap on the hall floor.

'Aaaagh!' she wailed. 'I've broken my leg!' Truffle came running, but didn't seem to notice the pain that his mother was in.

'Where's my lunch?' he said. 'I'm hungry.'

'Help!' she cried. 'Call me an ambulance!'

'You're an ambulance. Now get up and cook!'

She tried. Give Mrs Snuffle her due, she tried to stand up and create something tasty and nutritious from cheese and toast, but her leg couldn't support her weight and she collapsed again. So Truffle took £5 out of her purse and went out for fish and chips instead.

'You're a hypocrite!' he said, turning in the doorway. 'What sort of example do you think you're setting me, lying there on the floor like that, in the middle of the day, like a great big lazy lump!'

'Don't leave me,' whispered his mother, but the front door had already been closed.

✳ ✳ ✳

When Truffle came back, his mother was in traction and his father was in the garden, hanging out the washing. He was fuming.

'There you are,' he roared, his face flushing red. 'You and your piles of dropped clothes! How dare you leave your mother like that! She could have died.'

'I could have died of *hunger*, you mean,' Truffle replied cheekily, causing a reaction from his father the ferocity of which he had never seen before. It was an overheated-steam-engine-boiler of an explosion!

'YOU ARE A SELFISH LITTLE BOY, TRUFFLE!' he hollered. 'I WISH THE CLOTHES PIGS WOULD COME AND TEACH YOU A LESSON RIGHT NOW!'

His father's voice was so choked with fury that it came out as a high-pitched squeak. The resulting sound waves caused the air to vibrate so fast that the clothes line quivered. It sang like a mournful violin string and sent a spooky hum down the line. From one garden to the next, clothes lines trembled and passed on the sound of Mr Snuffle's voice, carrying his message into the countryside like a telephone cable.

When his voice arrived at Cherry Tree Farm, the four tiny piglets, Insy, Winsy, Nibble and Titch, were so hungry that they hadn't got out of bed for a week. They had started to wonder if they would ever eat again. So when they heard Mr Snuffle's despairing cry come down the wire they pricked up their ears and leaped to their feet.

'Problem in the Snuffle house!' cried Winsy. 'Call for the Clothes Pigs!' Insy and Titch cheered and sang a merry song . . .

'We're going to eat
We're going to eat
We're clothing up
For boy meat!'

. . . while Nibble rolled his eyes and sniffed the air. 'I smell Truffle!' he cried.

'And we do love truffles!' the brothers squealed as one.

The Clothes Pigs wasted no time in sorting out their affairs and setting off in a hurry for the big city, letting themselves out of the gate with a wave to Big Bertha and a collective grunt to their mother, informing her that they would be back soon.

'Whatever,' she replied. Unlike human beings, pigs are remarkably relaxed about letting their children get on with their lives.

❋ ❋ ❋

On the way to the big city, Insy, Winsy, Nibble and Titch stopped in .

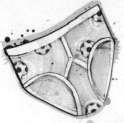

several gardens to pick up supplies. In the first garden they jumped into a peg trug sitting beside a washing line, wriggled down into the wooden pegs and waited until a woman appeared with a basket full of washing.

While she was choosing a shirt from the basket they lay ram-rod still, holding their front legs high above their heads as if frozen in the middle of a Mexican Wave, and their back legs stretched straight down like a ballerina on point. It fooled her. When the woman picked up a peg from the trug it was Nibble. He grabbed onto the washing line with his front trotters while she pushed the shoulder of the shirt into his rear trotters, picked up Insy and put the other shoulder into his.

Two minutes later, Winsy and Titch had joined their brothers on the line clutching in *their* trotters a splendid pair of brown corduroy trousers. When the woman went back indoors, they simply let go of the line, dropped to the ground and ran off with their booty.

And so it went on, from garden to garden. The four little piglets were picked up and pegged out on washing lines, until they had accumulated enough clothes to make one complete outfit.

And *this* was how they entered the big city without being seen: disguised as a human being, wearing brown trousers, a pink shirt, blue socks, a crew neck jumper, a thick woollen overcoat, a black Homburg hat, and sunglasses (which Titch had pinched off a table outside a pub). The Clothes Pigs made themselves the size and shape of a man by climbing onto each other's shoulders and forming a pig-pole. Nibble was the face – he wore the shades and had to do all of the talking. Titch drew the short straw and got the legs, while Insy and Winsy stood on his shoulders and provided an arm each. With every passing minute dinner came closer and closer. They walked through the town with a smile for every butcher and a wave for every passer-by . .

.

'Morning!'

'Morning!'

'Morning!' they cried, as they tipped their hat to the ladies. And nobody suspected a thing.

Least of all their dinner!

* * *

When the Clothes Pigs arrived at Truffle's house, Mrs Snuffle was resting and Mr Snuffle was weeding the front garden, so they were able to sneak in through the cat flap. On the mat inside the back door, they found a pile of Truffle's clothes lying exactly where he had dropped them a few hours earlier. Jumping down off each other's shoulders, they stripped off their stolen clothes, hid them in the coal hole in case a speedy exit was required, then slipped into Truffle's clothes. Just in time, as it happened.

'Who's there?' called out Truffle's mother from her sick bed. When there was no reply, Mr Snuffle came to investigate, but all he saw was a back view of Truffle sitting at the table hunched over a comic. He couldn't see his face or hair, because Truffle was wearing his hoodie, but it was definitely his son. Those were his clothes.

'Oh, it's you,' said Mr Snuffle. 'I thought I heard oinking.'

The Clothes Pigs had three hours to kill before Truffle came home. With nothing to do, their thoughts naturally turned to how hungry they all were.

'I'm famished,' squeaked Titch.

'I'm starving,' groaned Nibble.

'I'm *both*,' said Insy, who hadn't taken his eyes off the fridge for ninety-two minutes. 'Just a teeny-weeny snack,' he dribbled feebly. 'Please!'

'No,' said Winsy. 'You don't want to spoil your dinner.'

* * *

When dinner returned home from school at five o'clock, the Clothes Pigs snapped into action. It was vital that they were not spotted in the same room as Truffle lest Mr and Mrs Snuffle, seeing two sons, smelled a rat. If Truffle walked into a room, therefore, the Clothes Pigs shot out of the other door. Naturally there were mix-ups when the pigs accidentally ran into

Mrs Snuffles's bedroom and found themselves standing at the foot of her bed – but, luckily, her plastered leg (which was raised up in a harness) obscured her view. This meant that she never clocked Nibble's face.

She did, however, give them a scare when she asked suddenly, 'Why have you changed your clothes? When you rushed past my door a minute ago you were wearing something different.'

'Jam,' improvised Nibble. He had chosen the shortest word he could think of so that she had less time to realise that it wasn't her son's voice. 'Covered in jam!' Then he kicked Insy and Winsy's shoulders, which was the signal to scram, and they in turn kicked Titch's shoulders, who ran out of the room as fast as his little legs would carry them.

Watching Truffle eat his supper through a crack in the kitchen door was a painful experience. The pigs' stomachs gurgled and groaned as he ate his sausages.

'I wish he'd hurry up,' wept Insy.

'Patience,' said Nibble. 'Not long now.'

* * *

Finally, just before bedtime, the Clothes Pigs sneaked into Truffle's bedroom and hid under his bed, where they waited patiently for their dinner to be served. And waited. And waited. And waited. And waited.

'There's an awful lot of waiting being a Clothes Pig,' whispered Insy.

'But it's worth it in the end,' said Nibble, 'Ssssh!'

The shadow of the boy had just entered the room. Behind him, Truffle had left a trail of discarded clothes up the stairs. By the time he reached the edge of the bed, four pairs of piggy eyes had fixed him firmly in their sights. Their tummies rumbled as they gazed longingly upon their first food in a fortnight. He switched off his bedside light and climbed into bed. The springs creaked over the pigs' heads. They waited some more until Truffle had stopped fidgeting and started to snore. Finally, he was asleep.

'Ready?' whispered Titch, wiping his wet lips with the back of his trotter. 'Then let the eating begin!'

And the Clothes Pigs emerged from under the bed to a feast!

> In case you weren't paying attention earlier, pigs aren't fussy what they eat. Bone, gristle, ears, eyes, teeth, hair, toenails, they'll eat anything, right down to the buttons on a boy's pyjamas!

In the morning, the Clothes Pigs had gone . . . just like Truffle, in fact. They left the clothes they had borrowed in a heap by the side of his bed, and on the way home they revisited those gardens whence they had stolen their man-clothes, and hung them back up on the washing lines. Clothes Pigs may be many things, but they are not thieves. Then they returned to Cherry Tree Farm for a long sleep in the sunshine and to wait for their next invitation to dinner!

Your choice is simple; PICK UP or PIG! If you can't decide which one is for you just remember that picking up clothes can be very painful on the back, whereas being eaten by a pig is not painful at all. It's just a question of filling your head with pretty thoughts to take your mind off the pigs' teeth hacking hunks off you.

Oh, this is too much. I know I shouldn't, but he does go on!

'HEEEEEEEEEEEEEEEELP!'

Shall I tell you a secret?

Come closer. Don't be scared.

Really close. I'm not going to grab you or nibble your ear.

As close as you dare.

All the grown ups in the world work for me!

It's true! How do you think I know when you're being bad? I don't have allseeing eyes. I rely on my grown up spies!

WANTED
GROWN-UPS
who can bring up BAD CHILDREN

If you are a GROWN-UP who likes being
particularly unpleasant and can dish out
punishments without turning a hair,
this is the job for you.

Do something useful with your life.

Join the Hothell Darkness Recruitment Police!

<u>SPY</u> on your own children!

<u>SHOP</u> the offspring of friends and neighbours!

<u>CLEAR</u> the streets of bad children and earn
money while having fun!

FANTASTIC REWARDS

A world without children . . . for a start!
DON'T DELAY, BETRAY THEM TODAY!

Please display this poster in both the sitting room
window and the downstairs loo so that all passing
grown ups can see it.

Hello, again...

Some grown ups FIND naughty children and despatch them down here, dead or alive! Others turn GOOD children BAD. But most are under instructions to TEACH bad children a LESSON they will never ever ever forget!

How scary is that? It means you'll NEVER be able to trust a grown up again! Not at home, not in the street and certainly not at school!

These days there's a lot of old tripe talked about school dinners, about how school food was SO MUCH BETTER for children in the olden days when they drenched their bread in dripping and dipped their chips in ticker and horse fat. How much healthier it was, say the experts, when children ate brains for elevenses and lungs and lights for lunch; when children ate heart, kidneys, liver, intestines and testicles, and went back for more. They say that today's children that's YOU – are too sensitive to eat internal organs. That you grimace at guts and freak out at offal, which is why you eat nothing but chicken nuggets!

But *I* say, LET THEM EAT CHICKEN NUGGETS, because I know what goes into the making of them. One thing's for sure, it's NOT chicken!

Boo hoo! Boo hoo!

Dig-diggerdy-do!

Squeak! Squeak! Splat!

Bubble, bubble, bubble

SHUT UP! HOW MANY TIMES
DO I HAVE TO TELL YOU?

WHAT DID YOU SAY? SPEAK UP! I CAN'T HEAR YOU

I wan—I wan—I wan—I w—

JAMIE'S SCHOOL DINNERS

Jamie loved chicken nuggets. He loved all junk food, but chicken nuggets came top. He always said that if he was abducted by aliens and told that he could only eat one type of food for the rest of his life, he would choose chicken nuggets.

Other people, especially Mrs Saladbowl, the mother of Jamie's best friend Tom, thought Jamie was crazy. 'You want MORE chicken nuggets!' she gasped when Jamie went round for tea. 'Are you mad?'

'I love chicken nuggets,' dribbled Jamie.

'As a matter of fact, he *is* mad,' said Tom. 'It's the lack of nutrition in his diet, it's shrunk his brain.'

In fact, Jamie's brain hadn't shrunk, because it had never been big in the first place. Up until the age of three he hadn't had a brain at all, then his parents had given him theirs and now it was the size of two peanuts. They had made a ceremony out of it on a wet Sunday afternoon, going down on their knees and offering up their brains on a plush purple cushion.

'We want you to have these,' Jamie's father had said. 'We don't need them any more.'

'You can put our two little brains together,' his mother had whispered, 'to make one big brain.'

'I don't know what to say,' Jamie had said.

'Well, pop them in,' she had said, 'and maybe you'll think of something.'

Jamie's parents had stopped using their brains on the day they had explained to Jamie that a cola and a cheeseburger was a perfectly balanced meal.

'What do you mean by balanced?' he had asked.

'Well,' Jamie's mother had said, placing a cheeseburger in one hand and a can of cola in the other, then raising her arms until they were level with her shoulders. 'You can hold one in each hand, see. And because they're about the same weight it's balanced.'

'She couldn't fall over even if she wanted to,' Jamie's father had said. By now, Jamie's mother had eaten the cheeseburger and replaced it with a pound of lard.

'Actually, a pound of lard would balance too,' she had added.

'It would,' Jamie's father had said.

'Unless I went and ate it,' Jamie's mother had said, tearing off the paper with her teeth and licking the lard like ice cream, 'because I would, because I love lard!'

Even before they had given their brains away, Jamie's parents weren't the sharpest knives in the block. And now that Jamie had their brains he thought exactly as they did. It was hardly surprising, therefore, that he thought processed slops were delicious. He loved the taste, and because he wouldn't eat anything he hadn't tasted before, all he ever ate was junk.

And if it's true that you are what you eat that meant that Jamie was JUNK too, which is why, quite frankly, nobody cried when he disappeared. Because he DID disappear, under villainous circumstances!

By the time Jamie went to big school, he was a

huge, indolent lump. Eleven years of fatty foods had changed his shape. He was as round as a beach ball with skin so tight that he looked like an overstuffed sausage. His friends from primary school didn't want to hang out with him any more.

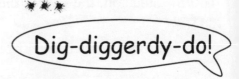

'Why?' said Jamie, stuffing his face with a cheesy chilli kebab.

'Because all you ever think about is food,' said Tom Saladbowl.

'And if any of us have sweets in our pockets,' added Bethany Bramley, 'you steal them off us and stuff them in your face without even asking.'

'I love sweets,' grinned Jamie.

'And if I'm sitting next to you on a bus,' chipped in Mini Milo, whose doctors were predicting a growth spurt any day now, 'you sit on me without even knowing I'm there. It's horrible!'

'Take the train!' slobbered Jamie, who didn't seem to care that he was losing his friends just so long as he never lost his taste for bad food.

* * *

Dig-diggerdy-do!

Jamie's fatness worried his new headmistress – a pernickety woman who hand-fed any pupil who wasn't eating five portions of fresh fruit and vegetables a day. She was a firm believer that healthy food built healthy pupils and healthy pupils did  better in the league tables. But of course she hadn't bargained on Jamie's stubbornness. The first time she tried to push a carrot between his lips he nearly bit her fingers off.

'I won't eat it,' he said. 'It's dirty!' The second time, she was more careful. She grated the carrot, held his nose and sprinkled it down his throat, but Jamie sicked it all up again and wiped his lips on her skirt.

The third time, she tried an altogether different approach. She burst into tears. 'Oh please,' she blubbed, sliding a chicken salad across the table to tempt him. 'Won't you at least *try* something?'

'You want me to try something?' said Jamie, defiantly.

'Oh would you,' she sobbed theatrically. 'For little old me.'

'All right, I'll try this—' he said, opening his

lungs and screaming at the top of his voice, 'YUCK!
IT'S DISGUSTING!' Then he hurled the chicken
salad against the wall and lowered his voice to a
snarl. 'Now do you believe I don't like it?' he said.

Jamie had made his point. The headmistress was
not going to win. But even if he wouldn't eat
healthy food, she still had a responsibility to see that
Jamie didn't starve. Accordingly, she phoned up a
dinner lady who advertised herself in the local
paper thus:

SCHOOL DINNER LADY FOR HIRE
I can't chop. I can't peel.
I can't cook.
Call Ambrosine to solve all
your catering problems.

Well, Jamie was a problem so it made sense to call
her. The headmistress was worried, however, by one
tiny thing. 'What do you mean, you can't cook?' she
said.

'Fresh food,' said Ambrosine on the other end of

the telephone. 'I can't cook fresh food, but I'm a whiz with chicken nuggets and a microwave.'

'You mean you can reheat junk?'

Ambrosine cackled with a laugh that sounded like a knife rattling in a ribcage. 'Yes, dear,' she wheezed, 'that's my skill. Reheating junk! It's so much less effort!'

And Jamie was JUNK, remember? You don't think, by any chance, that Ambrosine cooking Jamie's School Dinners might be a recipe for disaster, do you?

✳ ✳ ✳

The next day, during first break, an air horn cut through the chatter of voices in the playground and sent the children scurrying for safety. Seconds later, a huge silver tanker full to the brim with Fatty Fry's Cooking Oil pulled through the school gates and screeched to a halt on the five-a-side football pitch. The door to the cab flew open and a pair of black leather ankle boots jumped down on to the concrete. It wasn't the unnaturally curly toes or the long, icy black shadow that scared away the children, but the face. It was shaped like a crescent moon with a prominent chin and forehead, rotten

139

teeth and a hooked nose which had a single black hair protruding from the tip. It was the new dinner lady.

'You must be Jamie,' she hissed at the only child left in the playground.

'How did you know?' he replied.

'I can smell you,' she sniffed. 'Overweight children give off a powerful stench when they're ripe for the picking.' She took a small jar of white powder out of her pocket, unscrewed the lid, dipped in a teaspoon and licked off the sugar with a look of such eye-bulging rapture that she temporarily lost her footing.

'Careful,' said Jamie, steadying her with his hand. 'Are you the woman who's come to cook my dinners?'

'Don't touch me!' she snapped.

Jamie was unnerved by the coldness of her voice and took a step backwards. 'But don't you want to know what I like to eat?'

'It's obvious,' she spat. 'Now take me to your larder! We must feed you up immediately!' Which is exactly what she did.

✹ ✹ ✹

Over the next few weeks, Jamie grew fatter with every processed school dinner she shoved down his throat. Within a month her nickname for him was being chanted in the playground.

'Little goose! Little goose!
Too fat for chocolate mousse!'

But Jamie wasn't bothered by these taunts so long as the junk food kept coming. And come it did, by the bucketful! Each day brought a new surprise.

'These are bacon drummers,' said Ambrosine, handing a plate of what looked like chicken drumsticks through the serving hatch.

'Are these going to taste of bacon?' asked Jamie as he greedily snatched his lunch.

'They might do,' she said, 'but there again they might taste of fish.'

'So what are they?'

'Once they were legs,' she replied mysteriously.

'From a pig?'

'Unlikely,' she said, as he took a bite. 'Is it tickling your tastebuds?'

'It's delicious,' said Jamie. 'Tastes like old books. You know — paper and cardboard with a hint of ink.'

'More?' she twinkled.

'MORE!' he yelled greedily. This soon became the pattern for lunch. Not just firsts and seconds, but thirds and fourths as well, and Ambrosine only allowed him to leave the table when he was in actual pain from T.T.T. – Tummy Touching Table!

✷ ✷ ✷

Instead of turkey at Christmas she made him chicken nuggets shaped like feet. 'My signature dish!' she explained.

'What does that mean?' asked Jamie.

'This is the dish they all die for!' she squealed. 'Now go and sit down, my little goose. Today, in honour of my culinary genius, I shall serve you at table.' A few moments later, she emerged from the kitchen carrying a domed silver platter. Then, bowing low like a toadying waiter, she removed the lid and presented the feet for Jamie to sniff. 'Made from the rankest cuts that I wouldn't even feed to a dog,' she boasted, 'I have extracted all the taste and goodness, then pumped it full of artificial flavourings and preservatives to give this dish a shelf life longer than radioactive uranium.'

Jamie's eyes lit up. 'Is it chicken?' he asked.

'No,' she replied, 'but it would be chicken not to eat it. Enjoy!'

And a jolly stuffed Christmas he had too!

✳ ✳ ✳

As New Year turned into spring, Jamie gorged on fat, salt, grease, sugar and enough chemicals to raise the dead. It didn't matter what Ambrosine put in his food, Jamie ate everything, so long as it wasn't fresh. So when he found a radio receiver poking out of his chocolate pizza like a miniature Eiffel Tower, he didn't bat an eyelid. Down it went with everything else, battery pack and all.

But the junk food was taking its toll. After six months of solid eating Jamie was not only fat, with six chins and legs as wide as his waist, but now he was spotty as well. His face had erupted in a plague of yellow-headed zits and around his neck where the skin hung in folds like curtain swags, mushrooms had started to grow. The chemicals in Ambrosine's meals had mushed his brain so that he couldn't concentrate for more than five seconds at a time. He was lazy and forgetful, so much so that his parents never knew if he was coming home or not. On more than one occasion, Jamie found himself wandering the streets of a strange town trying to remember where he lived.

Mind you, Jamie's parents were just as bad as their son. They were both the size of barrels and because they ate the same junk food as Jamie every night, *their* memories were shot to pieces as well. Not only that, but their get up and go had long since got up and gone. It would be no exaggeration to say that the greatest misfortune in Jamie's life was having them as parents.

True. but none of us can choose our parents. can we? More's the pity!

✸ ✸ ✸

On one particular Tuesday morning, the listlessness in Jamie's house was as bad as it had ever been. Neither Jamie nor his parents had remembered their own names for a week. Jamie went off to school leaving his parents getting ready for work. When he returned home later that afternoon, he found them sitting in the hall with their coats still on.

'Hello!' said Jamie, walking through the front door. 'I'm . . .' There was a long pause while Jamie tried to remember what he was going to say. Eventually his father filled the gap.

'Home?' he said.

'No. Jamie,' said Jamie. 'I'm Jamie. I've remembered! Have you had a nice day?'

'We were going out this morning,' said his father, 'but we forgot where we were going, so we've just sat here instead.'

'Quite nice,' said Jamie's mother.

'I'm exhausted,' yawned Jamie, slumping to the floor for a kip.

This was her moment! Ambrosine's eyelids flickered as she half woke up. Then, brushing the cockroaches off her pillow, she dragged her twisted body out of bed and slapped in her teeth and eye.

* * *

Jamie was too tired to eat supper. While his parents sat up and watched a damp patch on the wall, thinking it was the television, he went to bed early.

'Phewwwww!' he sighed. 'All that remembering my own name has worn me out! Oh, I can see why,' he said, as he caught sight of his alarm clock, 'it's past my bedtime!' It was five o'clock in the afternoon.

One hour later, as sea-sick prawns splattered against the glass in the windows, a bell rang in a steel-ringed kitchen in the North Atlantic. From this she knew that Jamie was asleep. A crooked finger, dripping with pink gunge, switched on a radio-controlled transmitter.

✳ ✳ ✳

Hundreds of miles away, deep inside Jamie's stomach, the radio receiver burst into life with a high-pitched beep. His legs swung out of bed and his feet placed themselves on the floor. Then he stood up and started sleepwalking: down the stairs, out of the house and on to the street. He didn't wake. Not even when the driver asked him for his ticket on the night bus; not even when he stumbled across a runway in front of a jumbo jet; not even when the ferry left without him and he fell off the jetty into the cold North Sea; not even when the sharks circled as he swam the long, dark miles to the island . . . Ambrosine's Island, where junk food kids were junked!

By the way. I just happen to have six million ferry tickets to Ambrosine's Island. If you're a fan of junk food. see me afterwards.

When Jamie woke up he was lying on a wooden chopping board in the kitchen of a stone-walled castle. He was not tied down, but his head felt groggy and he couldn't move.

'Ohhh . . . I feel like I've been hit over the head,' he groaned.

'That'll be the monosodium glutamate,' said a familiar voice. 'It can leave some children with a bit of a hangover.'

It was a struggle to open his eyes, but when he did, Jamie saw Ambrosine standing directly behind him talking to someone on the other wall. He turned his head and saw a television camera.

'Where am I?' he mumbled.

'On telly,' hissed Ambrosine fiercely. 'This is a cookery programme for the Witch and Warlock Channel. So quieten down.'

Bubble, bubble, bubble

And you can shut up as well!

Best programmes on the Witch and Warlock Channel are *Witch of the Day*. *Strictly Come Broomsticking*. *Celebrity Ready Steady Stake-Burning* and *Dr Which*. I never miss them!

Duly chastened, Jamie watched Ambrosine turn back to the camera and smile. 'Next, you want to add plenty of salt and sugar,' she said, throwing a bucket of each over Jamie. The grains went up his nose and made him cough. She grabbed the back of his head and tugged him into an upright position, so that his back was straight and his mouth was forced open like the beak of a gosling at feeding time. 'Then simply add your stuffing!' she declared. 'That's three pounds of unrendered fat, bone and gristle, half a pint of blood, some e-numbers and a handful of unwanted eyelashes.'

She picked up a stainless-steel funnel and a basin of pink gunk, put the funnel into Jamie's mouth and forced the stuffing down Jamie's throat with a spoon. 'My good little goose,' she whispered under her breath. 'Now you're going to find out what meat I use in my chicken nuggets.'

Then she raised her head and once again

addressed the camera. 'And keep that going in until he's full. Now, this particular child shouldn't need much stuffing, because he's nice and plump already. So, tamp it all down . . . There we go. Last bit . . .'

Unable to move, Jamie had no choice but to suffer in silence. And suffer he did, because with every prod of her wooden spoon the stuffing was driven deeper into his body. As more stuffing went in he swelled and swelled and his skin grew tighter and tighter until finally it could stand the strain no longer. There was a moment of pain-free bliss and then he burst!

'And there it is,' she cried, as the kitchen rained Jamie. 'The fat child explodes!' Ambrosine was delighted with herself and hurried on to the next stage of her recipe. 'All you have to do now is scrape him off the walls into a mixing bowl and mould this gorgeous squidge into any shape that takes your fancy,' she said, taking a handful of Jamie out of the bowl and moulding it into the shape of a foot. Then she dipped the foot in breadcrumbs and dropped it into a deep fat fryer. 'That should take about twenty minutes. You'll know it's ready when it's burnt and inedible. And there we have it. What could be simpler? Perfect chicken nuggets, fit for the school dinner table, every time!'

Three days later, after the damp patch had dried out and Jamie's parents had nothing left to watch, they happened across their son's empty bed.

'Who sleeps here?' asked his empty-headed father.

'I don't know,' said his mother. They had completely forgotten that they'd ever had a son, which was lucky, because it saved them both from needless heartache. At 12.30 pm on that very same day, their son Jamie was served up on a plate to a gormless looking student in Scunthorpe, who ate half and scraped the rest into the slops bowl!

I went and had a look in that slops bowl but I couldn't tell which half got scraped in. All of Jamie is pink gunge now so there are no distinguishing features like arms or ears. And you. . . can't get a conversation out of him so you can't tell which end's got the mouth in. Still. I brought him back here and he lives in The Darkness now. I had a bit of grouting needed doing so I've put him in the shower room . . . in between the tiles!

And just in case you're wondering; YES. It's a very big wall and there's LOADS MORE grouting to do! So EAT UP, JUNKERS!

Throughout this book I shall be giving you helpful hints on how to deal with gruesome grown-ups. I shall entitle this advice Helpful Hints on How To Deal With Gruesome Grown-Ups.

Helpful Hints on How To Deal With Gruesome Grown-ups

1. RESPECT YOUR ELDERS
When a new dinner lady appears at your school and offers you chicken nugget feet and bacon drummers, you know what to do. Remember your manners: be polite to your elders and betters and accept the plate with a slight bowing of the head, a lowering of the eyes and a firm, but unchallenging 'Thank you'. Then eat it all up! And when you explode I'll see you down here for a shower. Looking forward to it. Splish splash!

Schools would be the best places for me to find bad children, were it not for the fact that teachers make the worst spies.

'Oh we can't spy on the children,' they whine. 'It would be a violation of the trust between teacher and pupil!' They CLAIM they don't know how to use a **thumbscrew** or administer a **Vulcan death grip** and they strongly disapprove of iron masks and the use of **maggots** in torture! Most teachers don't even know how to SPELL discipline let alone dish it out! It's pathetic. What DO they teach them at Teacher Training College these days?

Thankfully there are plenty of gruesome grown-ups in the support services. Librarians, for example, are made of much sterner stuff. It's all that reading they do. It fires their imaginations and gives them evil ideas! Take Dolly and Dot. They taught me everything I know about cataloguing. And I don't mean filing books. I mean nailing a cat to a log and pushing it down a river!

Oh, happy days!

SILENCE IS GOLDEN

Dolly and Dot were sisters first and school librarians second. They were gentle and grey-haired on the outside, but inside – underneath that sheen of carbolic, behind that puff of talcum powder, beyond the boiled sweets, the tissues and the tears shed for every dead dog – *inside*, Dolly and Dot were as twisted as a whelk-winkler's knife!

You can generally tell what a lady is like from the contents of her handbag.

If you don't believe me, take a gander at 'Her Majesty's Moley' on page 69 . . .

Dolly and Dot never left home without tissues and a lipstick, a telescopic blowpipe, a knotted silk garrotte and a vial of deadly poison extracted from the throat of the Slimy Green Toad of Tahiti!

They worked in the library of a school in Colchester, where the children were so noisy that a herd of flat-footed elephants in pink tutus could have danced past the building and nobody inside would have heard them.

Granted, *all* children are noisy (they only have two settings on their voice boxes: *full on* or *full off*) but the children at this school were so noisy that the teachers had to wear ear plugs to stop their ear drums from bleeding.

* * *

It was all because of one girl. Her name was Dolores Bellicose. She had a voice so loud she could stop a pack of greedy third-formers at twenty paces, which is exactly what happened in the playground after Tuesday Tuck Shop, when a gang of twelve of them, led by a foolhardy girl called Tiggy the Specs, had her Crew creep up on Dolores's bag of mint imperials with a view to pinching them. It would have worked, except one of them stood on a snail.

Dolores heard the crunch, span round and fired off her mouth like a machine gun. 'DON'T **EVEN THINK ABOUT EATING MY SWEETS!**' she bellowed.

The blast from her voice knocked the third-formers off their feet with the force of a hurricane, and deposited Tiggy the Specs on top of the science block roof.

It was because Dolores's voice was so loud that every other child in the school had to shout to be heard over her. This was what made this school in Colchester the noisiest in the world. For example, at lunchtime, a simple request like 'Pass the ketchup' would cause major structural damage to the dining room with sound waves registering twelve on the Richter scale.

'PASS THE KETCHUP!' That was Dolores.

Meanwhile Pete Tinker, who was sitting close to Dolores and was only trying to save his chips from the grasping fingers of Robbie Glottle, had to raise the level of *his* voice to remonstrate with the chip thief. 'OI! THOSE WERE *MY* CHI—'

But Dolores still hadn't got her ketchup, because nobody had heard her above Robbie. So *she* had to step up a notch too. 'PASS THE KETCHUP!'

Which meant that Robbie couldn't hear what Pete was saying.

'WHAT DID YOU SAY?' Pete repeated what he'd said by hollering back to Robbie.

'THOSE WERE *MY* CHI-'

Only to have his words drowned out again by an impatient Dolores. 'PASS THE KETCHUP!'

'I CAN'T HEAR YOU,'

Robbie yelled to Pete.

'PASS THE KETCHUP!'

'NOT YOU *HIM!*,' Robbie bawled at Dolores.

'WHAT DID YOU SAY?'

screamed Pete, who now thought that Dolores had been shouting at him all along and he just hadn't heard.

'KETCHUP!'

screeched Dolores. It was this particular word that broke all decibel records in the United Kingdom, shook the building to its core and plunged the dining hall into silence. And it was during this brief lull that the hurt voice of Pete Tinker finally made itself heard.

'There's no need to shout,' he said.

But there was. Dolores loved shouting. If she shouted loud enough it meant that *hers* was the only voice ever heard. It meant that everyone else had to stop talking and listen to what she was saying, which made her the most important person in the room. And the room in which she liked shouting best was, of course, the library, where silence was the golden rule and her voice sounded twice as loud as anywhere else in the school.

I love school rules, because children are always breaking them. And when they do it's my rules that take over. RULE NUMBER ONE — Dead or Alive! I'll take you any which way I can!

✳ ✳ ✳

It was on a Thursday that Dolores finally sealed her fate. She was late for her first lesson, which was Library. Without her there the rest of the class had no need to shout, so the first ten minutes passed in peaceful silence with everyone reading their books. At ten past nine the door burst open and Dolores entered like a whirlwind.

'WOTCHA!' she screamed as she spat her chewing gum into the dustbin. Dolly and Dot looked up from their novels and sighed.

'You're late,' said Dot.

'IT'S NOT MY FAULT!' bellowed the

girl. 'SO WOULD YOU HAVE BEEN IF YOU'D HAD A JOURNEY IN LIKE MINE!'

'Dolores,' said Dolly firmly. 'Sit down. We're trying to read our—'

'I HAVEN'T TOLD YOU WHAT HAPPENED ON MY JOURNEY YET!'

It was Dot's turn to try. 'Save it till later,' she said, but Dolores ignored her.

 'I WAS ON THE BUS, RIGHT, SHOUTING INTO THE EAR OF THIS *SELFISH* OLD MAN WHO WAS SITTING IN MY SEAT. "GET UP, GRANDAD," I YELLED. "GIVE UP YOUR SEAT FOR A LADY!"'

Dot tried again. 'Dolores, please!' But she got the same result.

'AND WHEN HE WOULDN'T GET UP, I SCREAMED TILL HE DID. LIKE THIS. *AAAAAAAAAAAAAAAAGH!*'

Dolly tried to interrupt. 'Dolores!'

'BUT, GET THIS, MY SCREAM SMASHED THE WINDSCREEN AND WE CRASHED INTO A HERD OF ELEPHANTS IN PINK TUTUS DANCING DOWN THE STREET!'

At that point Tamara Tapeworm joined in. This

was significant, because the introduction of another voice jacked up the level. 'I SAW THE ELEPHANTS TOO,' she cried.

'Children!' trilled Dot, trying to keep a lid on it, but the stew was out of the pot.

'ME TOO!' shouted Pankot Chumbawumba.

'AND ME!' bawled Barry Pew.

'AND ME!'

'AND ME!'

'AND ME!'

'Will everyone stop shouting!' Dolly tried to raise her voice to top the swelling noise, but didn't get close.

'DOESN'T ANYONE WANT TO HEAR WHAT HAPPENED AFTER THE CRASH?' hollered Dolores, thrusting herself back into the limelight.

'Quiet!' squeaked the two old ladies together. But even together their voices were no match for Dolores.

'QUIET YOURSELF!' roared the decibel queen. 'YOU TWO MAKE MORE NOISE THAN THE REST OF US PUT TOGETHER! HA HA HA!' And the whole class followed suit. When the class started laughing, Dolly and Dot knew that they had lost. 'HEY! LET'S TURN THE LIGHTS OUT!' yelled Dolores. 'THEN IT'S MORE LIKE READING IN BED.'

'YEAAAAAH!' came the mob's reply. As the lights went out all over the library, Dolly and Dot beat a retreat, leaving the children to scream until they were sick.

> What did you say? Speak up! I can't hear you...

> But we can hear YOU, Jumbo! And rather wish we couldn't.

✳ ✳ ✳

There is only so far you can push a librarian. And on this particular occasion, Dolly and Dot had been pushed **BEYOND THE POINT OF . . .**

NO REVENGE!

Dolly and Dot slumped into a couple of wobbly chairs in the cubbyhole that was laughingly referred to as their office. Dolly handed Dot a pair of scissors then removed the copy of *The Poisoner's Bible* from the top of the glass tank behind her head and handed her sister the crocodile.

'Oh, Dolly!' said Dot, as she clipped the crocodile's toenails.

'Oh, Dot,' said Dolly. 'Why won't they listen to us?'

'Because they can't hear what we're saying over Dolores, dear. We need to shut her up—' an evil thought flitted through her mind '—for good!'

'Ooh, Dot. I've just had an idea,' gasped Dolly, breathing out onto a brass knuckleduster and polishing it on her cardigan. 'Why don't we break Dolores into bits and file her away under T for tongue and F for foot . . . No, no, no! Even better! Nobody ever goes into the Ancient History section, we could file *all* of her in there.'

'Not sure that's such a good idea, Dolly dear. I think the police might want a word with us.'

'Quite right,' said Dolly. 'We wouldn't want to do anything illegal.'

'No, dear.' Dot took a moment to replace the crocodile in the tank and feed the tarantula. Then she pushed her teeth out through her lips and sucked them back into place with a slurp. 'What we need,' she said cunningly, 'is the help of an alchemist.'

'An alchemist?' said Dolly.

'A wizard who can turn things to gold.'

'Gold! Gosh!' Dolly was impressed. 'Why?'

'Because,' said Dot mysteriously, 'silence is golden.'

'Oh very good,' smiled Dolly, replacing the knuckleduster on the desk next to the eye-gouge. 'Very good indeed.'

It's a strange thing about eye gouges – now you see them, now you don't!

The two old ladies looked up 'Alchemist' in the *Yellow-Gold Pages* and found an evil genius on a quiet trading estate in Billerickie. 'Quiet' was perfect for what Dolly and Dot had in mind, and evil genius wasn't bad either.

Aaaaaaaaaaaaagh! This is a nightmare!

A bit of quiet wouldn't be bad, either!

The alchemist's name was Dr Calf. 'Bring her here to the laboratory and I'll do the necessary,' he said coldly, when the librarians had explained their problem. 'Anything else?'

'Well, yes,' said Dolly. 'What shall we do with Dolores once we've turned her into gold?'

'Good question,' said Dot. 'It seems a shame to waste her, doesn't it? Maybe, just for a change, we should turn her into something *useful.*'

'We could always melt her down into a necklace,' squeaked Dolly-the-psycho. Dot furrowed her brow. 'You know, Dolly dear, there is a cruel streak to you that I've never noticed before.'

'Is there, dear? Does it shock you?'

'Not at all,' laughed Dot. 'I like it!'

'We could always sell her.'

'And make money out of her. Yes! We could fund a little Silence Project for the library.'

'My word, what a splendid idea,' cried Dolly, 'a Silence Project. What perfect irony!'

'I'll have a word with some museum people I know in Mexico,' said Dr Calf, who was waiting to gold-plate a gerbil. 'We can flog her off as an old Aztec statue. Good day.' Then he steered the librarians out of his laboratory and sent them on their way.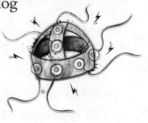

❋ ❋ ❋

Somehow Dolly and Dot had to get Dolores into Dr. Calf's laboratory without raising her suspicions. They decided that going by bus would be the best option as they could use their Over-60s bus passes and it wouldn't cost them a penny.

＊ ＊ ＊

The following Monday, on the pavement outside school, they separated Dolores from her friends with the help of a well-aimed wheelchair. Dolores had just said goodbye to everyone – 'BYE, EVERYONE!' – and stunned several pigeons out of a tree, when a runaway wheelchair caught her a stinging blow on the back of the knees. The force of it caused her knees to buckle and she had to sit down, whereupon the wheelchair whizzed her to the edge of the pavement, tipped up in the gutter and propelled her into a bus, where Dolly and Dot were waiting for her. They were slightly out of breath, having first given the wheelchair a shove, then run past it in order to be on the bus before Dolores arrived. She landed in the empty seat between them.

'Oh, there you are, dear,' said Dot, as if Dolores's

appearance was no surprise at all.

'ARE YOU TWO KIDNAPPING ME?' screamed the girl, trying to draw attention to herself.

'Ssssh,' whispered Dolly. 'Don't be silly, dear.'

'Do we look like desperadoes?' giggled Dot.

'BECAUSE IF YOU *ARE*,' persisted the world's loudest mouth, 'I SHALL SCREAM!'

'Not again, please!' begged the bus driver, brushing the remains of a pink dancing dress out of his face. It was snagged in a crack in his windscreen. 'I am still peering through this elephant's tutu from this morning!'

'No, dear. No!' said Dot. 'We're not kidnapping you. We're taking you to see a doctor friend of ours to measure the loudness of that pretty little voice of yours.'

'WHY?'

'Because,' said Dolly slowly, giving herself time to invent a good lie, 'we think you should be in the *Guinness Book of World Records*.' Dolores was impressed.

'*THE GUINNESS BOOK OF WORLD RECORDS*! BUT I'LL BE FAMOUS!'

'Yes, so we don't want you wasting your voice by screaming now. Understood?' Dolores nodded her head.

'Good girl!' said Dolly, flashing a sinister smile.

* * *

Once inside Dr. Calf's laboratory Dolores continued this run of good behaviour by saying very little. It probably had something to do with the straps around her jaw and the tin-plated helmet delivering 16,000 volts through her brain. Dolly and Dot heard an 'Ooh!' and an 'Ow!' and one final 'Ugh!' as the frothing girl was turned into gold. Then there was silence.

Later that night, a wooden box was dragged out through a back door of the laboratory and loaded on to a tractor. It was driven to the coast, where a merchant ship bound for Mexico City was waiting to depart. The box was loaded into the hold and the captain handed over a large wad of cash to the delivery team – two sweet old ladies and an alchemist.

And there the story should have ended, had the merchant ship not been hijacked by a band of cut-throat pirates, two of which had remarkably smooth skin for old seadogs. They had only just joined the ship under the names Dead-Eyed Dot and Dolly

Dogbreath. Anyway, during the transfer of the golden statue to their ship these two pirates, who had been ordered to hold on tight to the safety rope, 'accidentally' let it slip, and the statue plunged into the water.

'Whoops!' cried Dead-Eyed Dot. 'Butter fingers!' But it was too late to do anything about it. Hundreds of feet beneath the surface of the water, Dolores Bellicose was sinking like a silent stone.

She came to rest on the sea bed, where she still stands today, where not a strand of her golden hair moves in the current, where sharks brush past her metal skin, where an octopus sleeps on her head and where nobody, even if she could open her mouth, will ever hear her scream.

You won't be surprised to know that the school in Colchester isn't noisy any more. In fact the silence in the school library is more silent than the silence in the library of a Trappist Monastery. There's a good reason for this. Fear.

After their holiday, Dolly and Dot came back with one or two new ideas for their Silence Project. Now, if anyone talks in the library, or squeaks or burps or even *looks* like they might make a noise,

Dolly and Dot simply open the window and make them walk the plank.

Does the trick every time!

It's such a shame that I never got my hands on Dolores. I had her room ready and everything. It was a sound-proofed cell filled with round-the-clock ear pain; the cry of a hungry baby, the squeak of a piece of chalk scraped down a blackboard and the whine of a high-speed dentist's drill!

I expect I'll get letters of complaint now from dentists. Well, they can write as many as they like. I shan't reply. I don't write letters anymore. Not after I wrote one to that popular magazine that caters for badly dressed people who wear offensive clothing TANK TOP WEEKLY! and never got a reply.

Boo hoo hoo! Boo hoo hoo!

I hope that's not sarcasm, Poppy.

THE HOTHELL DARKNESS

Dear Tank Top Weekly!

It is high time someone asked the unaskable question. Can the elimination of a child for displaying an offensive taste in clothes ever be justified? In my opinion, the answer is a resounding YES. Today's children are too vain. They care far too much about what they look like. It's all 'OOH! LOOK AT ME, EVERYONE! I'M A REBEL. I'M SO COOL, BECAUSE I LOOK DIFFERENT FROM EVERYONE ELSE!' Well, take it from me, any child striving to look different generally ends up looking a MESSY MINGER! To this end I would recommend to you The Old Tailor of Pelting Moor who has helped me out more times than I care to mention. He is a uniquely evil old man who takes enormous pride in his work – namely stitching up vain children – and I cannot recommend him highly enough to your readership.

Yours etc etc

PS Obviously, etc etc is NOT my name. My name is a closely guarded secret. If I told your readership my name I would have to kill each and every one of them, and as your readership is in excess of three and a half million this might prove rather time consuming.

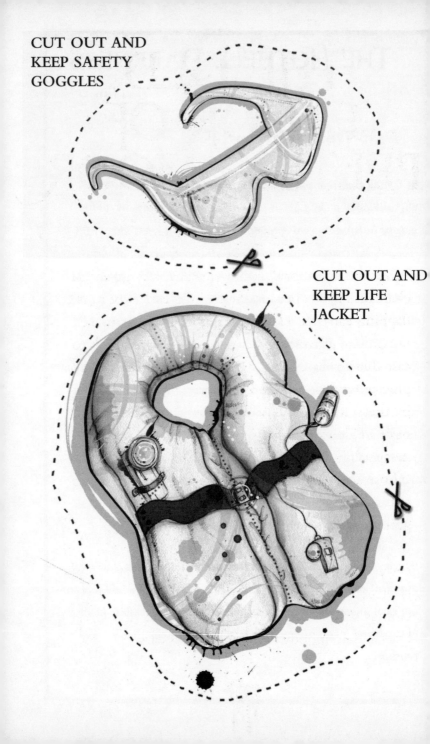

CUT OUT AND
KEEP SAFETY
GOGGLES

CUT OUT AND
KEEP LIFE
JACKET

THE OLD
TAILOR OF
PELTING MOOR

When he was born, Jumbo Ferrari was given an elephant's name, because he had big ears. Not huge flapping ears that caught in swing doors or picked up satellite signals, but ears that were big enough to cast their own shadow and frighten the life out of ping pong balls. While he was still a baby in his cot by the side of his mother's hospital bed he caught sight of these ears reflected in a kidney bowl and made a life-changing decision.

Those are such big ears, he thought, that I'm never going to be able to hide them with hair. I'm going to have to think of some other form of distraction to take peoples' attention away from them. His distraction of choice was clothes. He would wear clothes that were so outrageous and bizarre that nobody would notice his ears.

The following morning he threw the hospital blanket out of his cot and made it clear, by refusing to be wrapped in it again, that he did not want to wear the same as other babies. He only stopped crying when they wrapped him up in newspaper; so that was how he left to go home. By the time he was out of nappies, he would only wear clothes that did NOT go together – swimming costumes and Wellington boots, baggy shorts and long johns, frilly shirts and tank top jumpers. No item of clothing was taboo, so long as it made him look different from other children and distracted from his ears. He bought blouses from clothes shops for girls, four-legged coats designed for afghan hounds and dead peoples' clothes from the charity shop. He clashed colours and styles, while experimenting with hats and divers' boots, plastic macs and jewellery and sheepskin socks with tartan trousers. But above all, he gained a reputation for looking like the scary geek to avoid on the bus!

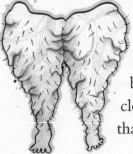

By the time he was eleven, however, what had started off as ear-distraction had turned into full-blown vanity. His bizarre style of clothing was more important to him than anything else in the world. As far as he was concerned, he was living his life at the cutting edge of fashion.

It wore his poor parents out.

In fact they were so worn-out that strangers who saw them on the street thought that they were Jumbo's grandparents. It was the grey hair, stooping shoulders and bungee cords of spit that bounced up and down from the corners of their mouths.

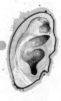

'Have you any idea how much all of these clothes cost us?' croaked Jumbo's mum one morning, when Jumbo walked into breakfast wearing an edible boiler suit trimmed with fake leopard fur, a pink rope belt and a gold baseball cap with the word GEEZER stitched across the front.

'Mama,' he replied, in the poor French accent that he'd cultivated to complement his image, 'when you are as big a fashion icon as *moi*, cost is an irritating irrelevancy!'

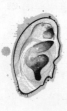

'To you maybe, but not to us!' grumbled his father, who was using a piece of burnt toast to black in the scuff marks on his shoes. 'Have you noticed by any chance that we don't have a bedroom?'

'You don't *need* a bedroom,' laughed Jumbo. 'You got it right first time when you made me. Why go through all that palaver again?'

'We haven't got a bedroom, because it's full of your clothes!' coughed his mother, clasping a stained, yellow handkerchief to her prunish lips. 'They're Piled up in front of the window. I haven't seen a sunrise for six years.'

'And whose fault is that?' cried Jumbo. 'Not mine. Buy a bigger house with an extra wing for my clothes and you can have your bedroom back.'

'You've spent all our money,' wheezed his father, returning to his favourite topic.

'So you'd have me going out in public looking like a chav?' cried Jumbo. 'It costs money to be one of life's beautiful people,' he added modestly. 'An expense, however, that is paid back by the many admiring glances I attract in the street.' To call them admiring glances was not strictly accurate. They were looks of utter, jaw-dropping disbelief.

There was no arguing with Jumbo's vanity. He was obsessed by how he looked. Clothes were obviously important, but so was his hair, which was restyled every fortnight; his moisturising routine, which included full nasal waxing and mud packs; and his freckles, which he bought from the Flipping Frinton Freckle Factory and stuck on every morning!

Whenever his parents pointed out that a life spent in thrall to vanity was a pointless and ultimately wasted life, Jumbo struck back with vitriol.

'At least I don't look like you two,' he said. 'Better to be vain than old and ugly!' His parents had never paid much attention to their clothes, even less now that they could not afford to buy them. They made do with practical brown cardigans and comfortable slippers, grey housecoats and slacks, or matching fawn anoraks with double-strength zips. They cut out the cold with car coats and warm woolly hats and preferred their colours dull to blend in with their dull lives. Their dress sense was exactly the opposite of Jumbo's, which is why he despised them.

But to despise one's own parents is a very dangerous game to play, because parents are programmed to correct the faults that they find in their children. They have no choice. It is the Grown-Up way. Jumbo's parents knew only one way to correct their son's vanity. They picked up the phone and made a person to person call: PELTING MOOR 4606.

I'm going to treat you to one of my famous songs now. Lucky you.

Kids who hate their parents
They are bad, bad, bad.
Falling out of love
With their mum and dad.
If the way they look annoys
And gets underneath your skin.
Then the only cure I know
Is to change the skin you're in!

It was no coincidence, therefore, that two weeks after this conversation with his parents, Jumbo saw an advertisement in a fashion magazine for a new type of suit.

The Unique Life Suit
The latest in bespoke craftsmanship from the Old Tailor of Pelting Moor

Every suit was tailored to the individual so it was different from every other suit ever made in the world. Jumbo *had* to have one. He scoured the page, but there was no contact address, no phone number and surprisingly no Pelting Moor on the map. So he tucked the advertisement under his pillow with the intention of tracking down the Old Tailor in the morning.

But that night he had a dream. In his dream, he was asleep in bed when he heard a noise in his wardrobe. It sounded like old bones rattling, followed by the flapping of leathery wings. Not the sort of noise you particularly want to investigate in the middle of the night, especially when the light switch is on the other side of the room. But, being a dream, in which the dreamer never does what common sense dictates, Jumbo got out of bed and opened the wardrobe door.

Slowly, of course . . .

Inch by inch . . .

Only to be knocked flat by the door bursting open and his beloved clothes jumping out! They stamped all over him as they danced across his bedroom like an invisible boy band, opened the window and threw themselves out. He rushed over to see where they'd landed, but there was no sign of them. His clothes had vanished and the cupboard was bare!

✳ ✳ ✳

Jumbo woke with a start. He was sweating all over. The thought of losing his beautiful clothes was enough to paralyse his heart! He gulped in a large pocket of air as a wooden groan span his eyes to the wardrobe. What he saw there made his pupils dilate.

'My clothes!' he wailed. 'Give me back my precious clothes!' It had been much more than just a dream. His wardrobe *was* bare.

Unable to believe his own eyes, Jumbo stumbled into the wardrobe to check for false bottoms and sides, but as he fell against the back panel, it gave way. It collapsed backwards under his weight and swung through the wall like a door. Jumbo fell through the hole into the shadows of a dark and silent room.

Buckle up! Here comes the gruesome grown-up!

It was a tailor's basement workshop. Through the narrow high windows on the back wall, Jumbo could see the faint shapes of legs walking along a pavement. The glass was grimy black and choked out the sunlight. The only lighting, therefore, came from two candles that flickered on the large central

table and threw the boiling shadow of a man on to the ceiling. Between the candles, as yet oblivious to the stranger watching him, sat a cross-legged old man sewing a piece of cloth. He had a bald head crowned by white, wispy hair, thick spectacles and a thimble on his finger. He also had the droopiest, flappiest, wrinkliest skin that Jumbo had ever seen. It hung off his bones like an old turkey's wattle.

'Ah,' he said suddenly, raising his red eyes. 'Is that Mr Ferrari? Welcome.'

'Who are you?' said Jumbo, still hugging the floor, as if somehow the flagstones were going to protect him from this wizened walnut of a man.

'The Old Tailor of Pelting Moor at your service, sir.'

'How did I get here?' asked Jumbo, cautiously.

'Never ask *how*,' winked the old man, easing himself achingly off his perch. 'The question is always *why*. You're here, my dear sir, for a life suit.' He slid open a drawer in one of the tall cabinets at the side of the table. 'Allow me to show you a demonstration one.'

He pulled out an all-in-one jumpsuit which, quite literally, jumped to attention and brushed itself down in front of Jumbo. It was made from one

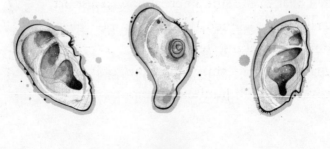

piece of cloth that shimmered like mother of pearl. A single cut it may have been, but it had been exquisitely tailored to look like a suit with a shirt underneath and separate jacket and trousers. Jumbo fell in love with it almost at once and couldn't stop himself from reaching out to touch it. 'Be my guest,' said the wrinkled tailor, reading Jumbo's mind.

He invited Jumbo to try the life suit on. 'It's beautiful,' said the boy.

'And not another like it in the world.'

That was what Jumbo wanted to hear. With his own personal life suit he'd be one of a kind!

* * *

The material hugged his body in a way that no other material had ever done before.

'It's so light,' gasped Jumbo. 'It's as if I wasn't wearing anything at all.'

The tailor laughed. 'Some people do say it's like wearing a second skin,' he said, brushing a small sprinkling of dandruff off the collar of the suit. There followed a short period of silence while Jumbo gazed adoringly at his reflection in a cracked mirror. During this pause the old tailor moved behind Jumbo to smooth down

the back of the life suit. As he took his first step, however, he tripped over the skin on his legs, which had collapsed over his ankles like a baggy old pair of woollen tights.

Jumbo paid no attention as the old man struggled back to his feet. Instead he smiled and said, 'It makes me handsome!'

Suddenly, in the mirror, the face of a complete stranger flitted across his own. It happened so quickly that Jumbo questioned whether he had seen it at all. 'Who was that?'

'Who?' said the tailor distractedly.

'The boy whose face just flashed across mine.'

'Oh, him,' said the old man. 'That was nobody. Just the face of the boy I made the suit from.'

'Made it *from*?'

'*For*! Made it *for*! Goodness me! Slip of an old man's tongue! So—' he added, steering off the subject quickly '—does sir want me to make him a life suit of his own?'

'Yes,' grinned Jumbo. 'Sir *does*!'

* * *

Dig-diggerdy-do!

I won't tell you about the noise again. Mattie. If you want me to get the big spade out. I can!

The Old Tailor of Pelting Moor measured Jumbo from head to toe then politely asked him to step out of his skin.

'I beg your pardon?' chuckled the boy, thinking that this was an old tailor's joke.

'Did I not mention it?' mumbled the old man. He seemed distressed. 'Old age is such a curse. If it's not more wrinkles, it's less memory. Now, where was I? Oh yes. The reason why the life suit is 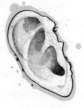 unique is because it's made from the wearer's own skin.' Jumbo suddenly realised what that meant. 'So that face was the face of the boy whose skin I was wearing?'

'Alas poor Yorick, I knew him well! It's a time-honoured process. First, I strip off the skin, which is lovingly preserved in unguents and oils to prevent

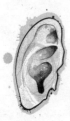 ageing. Then I nip and I tuck and I might even snip a bit too to achieve the final look.'

'You're a plastic surgeon,' said Jumbo.

'Hardly, sir. The most skilful tailor in the world.' There was a flash of fury in

183

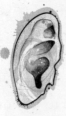 those rheumy eyes that Jumbo thought not to challenge.

'Very well,' he said, ignoring the side of his brain that was flagging up danger. 'And how exactly do I step out of my skin?'

'That is why we have ears, sir – in your case, quite large ones – to hide the carbon fibre poppers. Hold still and I'll have you out of there in a jiffy.' Then he leaned forward, popped off Jumbo's ears and revealed two red tags underneath. Each had a tiny label attached – **PULL TO RELEASE** - which is exactly what the old tailor did. Two sharp tugs and Jumbo stepped out of his skin like a work-experience ghost lifting off its white sheet.

✻ ✻ ✻

All that night, Jumbo sat up in a chair in his bedroom and listened through the holes in the side of his skull to the old tailor working in the wardrobe. He wrapped a blanket around his shoulders to keep himself warm, for without a skin Jumbo was nothing more than a collection of bones, and cold draughts like nothing more than ribs to whistle through.

In the morning, Jumbo could barely contain his excitement as he and his bones clattered into the wardrobe to try on his Life Suit. He saw it immediately, hanging loosely on a peg, but the old tailor was nowhere to be seen. Without asking permission, Jumbo tried it on.

'Good morning, sir. How does it fit?' asked a familiar voice from behind him. Jumbo neither replied nor turned round, for at that precise moment he was popping back his second ear and lifting his head to admire his new suit in the mirror. As his eyes hit the glass he gasped and clutched his mouth. In his worst nightmares he had never imagined it looking like *this*.

The suit was appallingly made. It bore no resemblance to the demonstration model he'd been shown. The trousers were ragged shorts, the jacket covered less shoulder than a scarf and the shirt looked like a stretched, overworn T-shirt. And hanging out from beneath the clothes were folds and folds and folds of old man's skin. Loose and drooping, saggy and wrinkled!

'What have you *done* to me?' howled Jumbo, turning round to confront the old tailor – but the shocks just kept coming, because the tailor wasn't  old any more. He had young, firm skin and fine, chiselled features. Admittedly, he had only one ear, but everything else about the old tailor looked radiantly youthful. 'That's my skin!' stammered Jumbo. 'You're wearing my skin, and I'm wearing . . .' He looked down at his flapping body and burst into tears. 'These hideous wrinkles!' he cried. 'You've turned me into you!'

'It's not so bad,' smiled the tailor. 'You'll get used to tripping over the folds of skin when you walk downstairs. Word of advice, though – if you go cycling, you'll need to hitch the wrinkles up above your knees with bicycle clips, and don't go outside in a bathing costume if there's a high wind. Your arm skin will inflate like bat wings and you'll take off.'

Jumbo could not believe what he was hearing. 'But apart from that,' added the tailor, 'your life won't be that much different.'

'Won't be different!' choked Jumbo. 'You're an old crook! You've stolen my beauty!'

'Precisely,' said the tailor without a hint of a smile. 'Vanity in one so young deserves wrinkles. And at my great age, I rather think I deserve a facelift!'

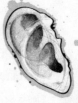

Oh, he is good!

And with that, the *young* tailor of Pelting Moor took his other ear out of his pocket, pressed it on to the popper on the side of his skull and vanished, along with his workshop, leaving Jumbo Ferrari standing in the middle of his bedroom with no other option but to face the rest of his life wearing an old man's saggy, baggy skin!

✳ ✳ ✳

From that day on, Jumbo went out in public only when he absolutely had to, but never to buy himself clothes. Cutting-edge fashion just didn't suit Jumbo any more. His parents, who suddenly had spare money to put aside for their old age, thoroughly approved of the change in their son.

'Not so chic now,' grinned his father.

'No,' sniggered his mother. 'Not with skin designed by Jumbo the Elephant!'

I'm glad to report that a few months later. Jumbo DID go out in a high wind wearing only a bathing costume and DID take off. He was up there for weeks, floating around the world on a Trade Wind. When he came down, he came down rather too hard, and made a hole so deep that he ended up on my doorstep.

I've put him in the Old Folk's Wing with other ancient children. It's rather sweet. The old dears have called it DUN LIVIN'. He's got his own room with his own coffin where the bed should be, and he spends his days sitting in a high-backed chair wearing a nice brown cardigan and comfortable slippers. And if he goes out he wraps up warm in a practical fawn anorak with a double-strength zip. Just like his father in fact! The father he once, rather foolishly, despised! What did you say? Speak up. I can't hear you!

Just listen to the old man go on. You go back to sleep, Jumbo. I'll be round in a minute with your medication.

Isn't it spooky the way children ALWAYS end up looking and behaving like their parents?

HER MAJESTY'S MOLEY

There was barely room to move. Certainly not backwards. The sides of the tunnel scraped every sinew of his body as he squirmed forward, coat damp and slick, blindly digging a path towards the perimeter. A noise up ahead made him stop and cock an ear. A soft thump, like a mouse falling on to dead leaves. But it wasn't a mouse. It was bigger than a mouse. It rolled towards him and bumped into his head. It was metal-hard with a pitted surface and a chain, which he nuzzled. Sniffing for a clue to its identity, he found the hole where the pin had once been. But that was all. As he

flicked out his tongue to taste the object, it revealed itself in all its brutal horror. In a flash he was dispatched into a silent storm, splattered into a white hot furnace of oblivion.

> **Don't eat me again! Please don't eat me again!**

> Ignore it. That's just the tiles talking!

'My turn! My turn!' squealed the little girl in the garden above. 'Can I drop a hand grenade into the mole's hole now?' She and her father were standing next to a smoking hole in a lawn that was blistered with molehills.

'No,' said her father. 'In a year or two. But, if I can just find the little blighter . . .' He knelt down, thrust his hand into the hole and, after fumbling around, produced the dead digger like a rabbit from a hat. 'There. If you want to hold it, I'll take your photograph.' Then he snapped away while the mole's battered body stained the grass red with its sticky drips. 'Say cheese!' her father cried. 'Smile!' The camera clicked. 'Now it's your turn to take me.' They always took a photograph of each other for the family album.

* * *

The girl was six years old, and wore a pinafore dress

and muddy red wellingtons. Her name was Mattie and ever since she'd been old enough to ask if she could join him, her father had taken her out on Mole Hunts. He was forty-eight years old, grey-haired and dressed for hunting – rifle over his shoulder, spade in hand and a quiver strapped across his back with rockets poking out.

Mattie and her father were like two peas in a pod. They both loved killing moles. To be fair, a hand grenade was not Mattie's father's preferred weapon of mole destruction. It was just that on this particular morning, he had happened to find one in the potting shed.

Normally, he and Mattie would leave home early in the morning before the moles were awake, drop loudspeakers down their holes and pump Drum and Bass through the tunnels until the moles were driven mad by the noise and ran out clutching their ears. Then he'd bash them on the head with a spade.

'Me next! Me next!' Mattie shouted keenly every time, but her father drew the line at spade work.

'It's too violent for a little girl like you, Mattie. Have a rocket instead.'

And so it was, from an early age, that Mattie

became expert at positioning firework rockets in mole holes, lighting the blue touch paper and retiring, safe in the knowledge that when you put a rocket up a mole there tends to only ever be one winner.

❋ ❋ ❋

On this particular morning however, having slung the grenade-splattered mole on the compost heap, Mattie was handed her first rocket of the day and told to 'Go bag another!'

Unfortunately, her rocket missed its mark. Instead of killing its intended target it caught the mole a glancing blow and maimed it instead. When Mattie's father reached into the hole to pull out the body all he found was a severed front paw. 'Never  mind,' he said, consoling his weeping daughter. 'You won't miss every time! Let's see if we can't make something special out of this.' And he took the paw back to his potting shed and turned it into a souvenir key-ring.

'Keep this always, Mattie,' he said, stooping onto one knee and pressing the keyring into her tiny hand. 'Let it be a permanent reminder of our mole-mangling days together.'

'Oh I shall, daddy,' she wept. 'I shall call it Moley and whenever I stroke its soft, silky fur I shall remember all the blood we've spilled together!'

❦ ❦ ❦

What neither of them realised was that the poor owner of the paw was still very much alive and had limped to the hole of a mole doctor – that's doctor as in *witch* not *medicine* – and knocked on his door. The mole was holding his injured paw across his chest and breathing heavily when the door was opened by an elderly mole wearing a grass skirt and spectacles. He had a feathered necklace around his neck, bracelets of teeth around his wrists and a small bone through his nose.

'Good morning,' he said in a well-to-do tone. 'How may I help you? Exorcism, curse, voodoo doll or haunting?'

The three-pawed mole came to the point. 'Do you do revenge?' he asked.

'Ooh yes,' said the doctor. 'I love a good revenge.'

'Excellent.'

'Do come in.'

'Thank you.' But the injured mole hesitated on the door step. Then, with an awkward forward thrust of his stump he mumbled apologetically, 'Normally I'd shake your hand, but I haven't . . . erm . . . Sorry.'

The witch doctor waved formality aside and took his visitor through to his witch surgery where they threw some magic bones and cursed cruel Mattie and her equally cruel father to a horrible end.

* * *

For those who have never come across such a thing before, the Curse of a Mole is rarely instantaneous. This meant that Mattie lived blissfully unaware of it and carried on blowing up moles without a care in the world until she was eleven years old. The curse kicked in on the day of her father's accident. He took a swing at a mole's head with his spade, missed and hit his foot.

'Noooooooooo!' she cried as she watched the leading metal edge slice through his combat boots. 'Daddddddddddddy!'

For his part, Mattie's father kept it short and sweet. 'Ow!' he said. 'That hurt.'

He died, three weeks later, from gangrene.

This was the end of the first part of the mole's revenge.

✳ ✳ ✳

Two hundred million people watched his funeral. It was a bigger than average turnout, but then he was not just Mattie's father, he was the prime minister of Great Britain as well. The funeral was a sumptuous affair, televised across the globe in twenty-five different languages, with eulogies showered on his cold head by statesmen from the four corners of the earth.

This tale should really be called The Tale of Two Dead Paws, shouldn't it? You'll like this. Dead Paw Number 1 was the three-pawed mole's dead paw, which was blown off by a rocket. Dead Paw Number 2 was Mattie's dead paw, who was the prime minister. Gettit?

Mattie's father was greatly missed by everyone; everyone that is except moles; and one mole in particular. Old Three-Paws himself!

✳ ✳ ✳

'Now,' he said, as he watched the late Prime Minister's coffin being lowered into the ground, 'let the second part of my revenge commence!'

'You're the boss!' said the witch doctor, draining his cup of tick-blood tea and switching off the television with the remote control. 'Hold this, will you?' He gave his cup to the three-pawed mole and squatted in the middle of the room. Then he closed his eyes and invoked the evil spirits of the Holy Moleland with a chant that he'd Googled off the internet. '*Humma hoinnng . . . oing . . . oing . . . oing!*'

When the witch doctor had finished chanting for the second part of the mole's revenge, the three-pawed mole left to do his duty.

'Are you sure you know the way?' asked the witch doctor. 'I've got an Underground map on the shelf somewhere.'

'No need,' said the three-pawed mole. 'I should be able to find Downing Street with my eyes closed.'

'And you're sure you know what the key-ring looks like?'

'It is *my* paw,' said Old Three-Paws. 'See you later.' And he waved goodbye with his stump.

'Cheerio,' said his fellow conspirator. 'And good luck!'

It was only after the funeral was over and the guests had filed out of 10 Downing Street that Mattie noticed it was missing. She was clearing up the house with her mother when she spotted that the trinket box under her bed was empty!

'Someone's stolen my precious Moley!' she cried. 'What will I sniff when I suck my thumb now?' The house was turned upside down, but the mole's paw key-ring could not be found. After one whole hour of searching, her mother took Mattie to one side and whispered something secret in her ear.

'After the speeches,' she said, 'I was coming upstairs to find Elton John – I was going to ask him to sing us another sad song – when I saw someone slipping out of your room.'

'The thief!' gasped Mattie. 'Who was it?'

Her mother looked around nervously. 'The

Queen,' she hissed. 'Now, I know that the royal family is having to make big changes to keep up with the times, but I don't believe she's changed into a burglar. I mean, generally speaking, queens aren't that interested in stealing.'

'No,' said Mattie. 'But dogs are.'

'You're right!' gasped her
mother. 'Now that you mention
it, I remember that the Queen
was followed out of your
bedroom by six corgis, and the
last one looked decidedly shifty.'

'I saw it too,' said Mattie, 'in the hall as they were
leaving. I remember thinking, that's a strange-
looking corgi. It looks more like a mole! Gosh, I
think we've cracked it. I bet that's our thief; the
strange looking corgi at the back!'

'Not so fast,' cautioned her mother. 'We can't just
go around accusing the Queen's corgis without
proof. She could have us clapped in irons for the
rest of our lives.'

'Then we'll just have to *get* proof,' said Mattie.
'We'll just have to search the Queen's Palace until
we find that key-ring.' But getting in to
search a queen's palace is not as easy as it
sounds.

* * *

Meanwhile, two revenge-crazed
moles were sitting opposite each
other in the witch doctor's surgery.

The witch doctor mole was writing on a piece of ivory-coloured card with a quill pen. He curled the last 'h' of Elizabeth, then sat back and pushed the finished document across the table to Old Three-Paws.

'All done,' he said. 'One forged invitation inviting Mattie to the Queen's forthcoming garden party. Careful not to smudge the ink!'

The three-pawed mole was deeply impressed. 'Is there anything you can't do?' he asked.

The witch doctor pointed to the silver box in the corner of his room. 'I'm not very good at setting the video,' he said.

* * *

At three o'clock the following morning, a very short postman with a pronounced limp delivered a letter to Mattie's house. When Mattie opened her royal invitation she could not believe her good fortune.

'Sometimes, I think I've got a fairy godmother,' said the murderer of moles. 'I mean, how lucky am I? One day I really want to get into the Queen's palace to conduct a search for Moley but I don't know how,

199

and the next I get an invitation to a royal garden party!'

HRH The Queen Invites YOU

Mattie Bleurgh

2
A Royal Garden Party
At
The Palace
When? Next Week!
Bring a bottle

Mattie and her mother were dolled up to the nines when they arrived at the palace for the garden party, but Mattie never saw the garden. She snuck inside and spent her time dodging security while she hunted for Moley. She looked everywhere, from dungeon to tower, from banqueting hall to throne room. She checked behind portraits, suits of armour and gun racks. She turned out wine cellars, servants and boxes of old toys. She looked under the corgis, inside liveried footmen's footwear and behind old Beefeaters from a bygone age. But nowhere did she find it.

Then, just as she was leaving, she happened to glance at the hall table where the Queen's car keys were lying in the Queen's car-key bowl. And there it was. Soft, smooth, silky-grey and bloodstained with happy memories!

❦ ❦ ❦

'Excuse me, miss.' The beefeater had crept up behind Mattie while she was slipping Moley into her pocket.

She hadn't noticed he was there. 'Sorry?' she said, suddenly waking up to the danger.

'I believe you've got something there that belongs to Her Majesty.'

'No,' Mattie lied. 'Are you accusing me of theft?'

'A key-ring, perhaps?'

'I don't know what you mean. My daddy was a prime minister.'

'And my daddy was a thief,' said the beefeater, 'which is why I'm so good at catching them.'

Mattie was charged, tried and sent down for three years, to a correctional institution for naughty children. One week into her sentence, she was already bored and complaining that she had nothing to do. After a childhood spent blowing up moles with fireworks, prison life seemed a little tame by comparison. So imagine her delight when one of the warders announced that she had a visitor.

'How unexpected,' said Mattie.

'You can say that again,' said the warden. It was the Queen.

***

Helpful Hints On How To Deal With Gruesome Grown-ups

3. THE QUEEN

In 'Silence Is Golden', you found out that you can tell what a lady is like from the contents of her handbag. But this does not apply to the Queen. Do NOT look in the Queen's handbag to see what sort of lady she is or you will find out quicker than you think. She will have you arrested by a small army, hung, drawn and quartered on live TV, and fed to the ravens in the Tower of London. OK?

They sat on Mattie's bed and talked like old friends.

'One used to strangle moles oneself, you know,' confessed the Queen. 'when one was a princess. So one is familiar with the lovely smell and feel of moleskin.'

'I can't live without it, Your Majesty.'

'No. And for that reason one is granting you—'

Mattie jumped up excitedly. 'Not a pardon!' she shrieked.

'No. Not a pardon—' Mattie sat down again '—another chance,' said the Queen.

'Oh,' mumbled Mattie, as the Queen reached into her handbag and took something out.

'One wants you to have this,' she said, pressing a small, warm object into Mattie's hand.

'It's Moley!' she cried.

'Yes,' said the Queen, 'and you can keep it!'

'Are you sure?' gasped the prisoner.

'Well, it was yours to begin with, dear . . . and don't look so surprised that one should know. One extracted a confession from the corgis. Apparently a rather brazen mole infiltrated their number without them knowing and left it on my pillow.' She stood up and walked towards the door. 'So, is one happy?' she asked, even though she already knew the answer. She had only to look at Mattie's beatific smile, as she sniffed the fur and rubbed the silky soft paw across her cheek, to realise that the next three years were going to fly past for this happy girl.

What the Queen was not telling Mattie, however, was that she no longer wanted to keep Moley. Every morning since the accursed thing had been in her possession, strange things had been occurring to the royal face! Things that could be traced back directly to the curse of a certain three-legged mole!

* * *

Old Three-Paws switched on the witch doctor's video recorder and slipped in a tape.

'You mean a curse can sometimes overspill and affect others?' he said, selecting the Sports Channel.

'Only if they're guilty of the same offence,' said the witch doctor, settling into his favourite armchair and dragging it round to face the telly.

'There.' The three-pawed mole handed the remote control to its owner. 'That's got it working.'

'Excellent. I can record the cricket now.' Then the witch doctor mole pressed RECORD with his four fat fingers and hit FAST FORWARD instead.

For three years, Mattie lay happily in her prison cell snuggled up to Moley. For three years, the soft grey fur never left the skin on her face. For three long years she was blissfully unaware of The Curse of the Old Three-Paws. Then, come the day of her release, she was told to smarten up her appearance before stepping outside and, for the first time since she had been locked up, she was given a mirror.

It was a cruel way to find out. As Mattie raised the mirror to her face she did not recognise herself. Her face was covered in mole-coloured fur! She screamed and dropped the mirror, but as it hit the floor the angle of the glass revealed an even worse truth. It was not just her face that was furry; the curse of Old Three-Paws had covered her whole body in moleskin from the top of her head to the tips of her velvety toes!

'I'm a mole!' she cried. 'Dig-diggerdy-do!'

But that was not all. When Mattie the mole maimer went home she was so ashamed of the way she looked that she refused to let her mother see her. She ran into her bedroom, ripped up her floorboards, jumped into the hole and started digging to get as far away as she possibly could from the light.

Little did she know where she was heading. Suffice to say that the final part of the curse condemned her to live underground for ever in The Darkness!

THE CURSE OF OLD THREE-PAWS

I CURSE YOU, MATTIE BLEURGH, TO LOSE NOT ONLY YOUR PRECIOUS FATHER (PART 1) BUT YOUR PRECIOUS MOLEY TOO (PART 2) AND TO BE SO ANXIOUS TO GET IT BACK THAT YOU WILL COMMIT A CRIME FOR WHICH YOU WILL BE BANGED UP LONG-TERM. THIS MEANS THAT FOR THREE YEARS YOU WILL ONLY HAVE MY SEVERED PAW FOR COMPANY (PART 3). THREE YEARS OF CONTACT WITH MY DEAD FUR _AND_ NO MIRRORS! THAT SHOULD DO IT. AND WHEN IT'S DONE, IT'S THE DARKNESS FOR YOU (PART 4).

She arrived at Main Reception after
sixteen days of non-stop digging, and now
lives in a network of tunnels that I'd
specially prepared for her under Rooms
101, 102, 103, 104, 105, 106, 107, 108
and 109. When YOU come to stay
maybe you can play with her. You'd
enjoy a game of Hunt the Mole, and
I'll provide the giant rockets!

By the way, if ever you should ever happen to be
lurking outside the Queen's bathroom and hear
electric shaving from within, accompanied by an old
lady's voice cursing her
whiskers thus;

'Be gone foul moleskin!'
Now you'll know why!

Next time you look at
a stamp or a five pound
note see if you can spot
the difference.

Now, take a look at this
photograph.

As you can see. It is the photograph of a girl and her parents. Nothing unusual in that. except that where else would you find a daughter who was older than her parents? The photograph was taken in 1965 when the parents were six years old and best friends at primary school. The daughter was snapped thirty years later when she was eleven. And here's another strange thing; the parents are smiling whereas the girl is not. But I don't want you feeling sorry for the girl. Punishments are never handed out without just cause and in this girl's case there was cause aplenty!

THE SOUL STEALER

Poppy was a vicious gossip-monger who owned not one, but *six* mobile phones so that she could conduct simultaneous six-way conversations with her six brainless best friends. They would blather from morning till night. From the moment her pretty empty little head woke up, through breakfast, break and lunch, and for the whole six hours between school ending and bedtime starting, Poppy's mouth spouted rumours and lies till her lips were numb!

So greatly did her parents hate this mindless chatter that they came up with a cruel but cunning scare tactic to wean their daughter off her phones. It was breakfast time one morning, and Poppy had just spent forty-eight minutes discussing the colour of her socks with Millie, Molly, Mickey, Mandy, Dreena and Ash while her bacon got cold.

'You do know what mobile phones *do*, don't you?' said her father, the second after she'd hung up. 'Recent scientific research has proved that mobile phones microwave brains!'

Poppy's mother gasped theatrically. 'Imagine what must be happening inside your head, Poppy! Think of all that damage you're doing to your brain by using *six* phones all the time!'

'I wouldn't be surprised,' continued her father, laying on the horror with a trowel, 'if your brains hadn't been microwaved into scrambled egg by now!'

'Not poached, not boiled, but *scrambled*!' echoed her mother. 'Next time you put your head on one side your brain'll dribble out your ear!'

Poppy had a nightmare vision of sitting in a cinema and putting her head on her boyfriend's shoulder (prior to a smooch), only to find that scrambled egg was pouring out of her ear and dripping down his shirt!

'I know what you're doing,' she scoffed. 'You're trying to stop me gossiping by splitting me up from my phones. Well, here's some fresh gossip. You've *failed*! I'm not getting rid of them.'

'Not even if we were to replace all six with a

Nokisson 5000?' Poppy's father was fiendishly clever. The Nokisson 5000 had a digital camera. It was the all-singing, all-dancing, must-have mobile that every child wanted!

* * *

Twenty-four hours later, Poppy had swapped six mobiles for one. Instead of improving her 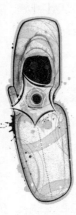 behaviour, however, the N5000 simply made it worse. It was no longer the witless chattering that caused the problem, it was the camera. The camera made Poppy smug and conceited, because amongst her circle of school friends it made her the centre of attention. Everyone wanted their picture taken. In the playground, girlfriends clamoured around her and fought each other for a glimpse of the lens.

'Me, Poppy. Me!' they screamed.

'Ow!'

'Get off my pigtails!'

'Over here!'

'CHEESY CHEESE! My smile's the biggest!' You'd have thought none of them had ever seen a camera before!

They'll see a camera when they get down here that's for sure. It's the one I use to take mug shots of all of my guests. It's called a Single Reflex Griffin. It's got the head of an eagle and the body of a lion. so when I tell my photographic subjects to 'Watch the birdie!' what I really mean is; 'Watch OUT for the birdie. because it hates children who wriggle and will rip out your throat if you don't sit still!' That's why it's called a Single Reflex. because that's the only reflex it knows.

One girl *hated* the camera. She was new to the school and her name was Ana. She had lost both parents in a holiday accident whilst photographing them in front of a cable car. One minute they were there, the next they had gone. The police enquiry concluded that they had slipped over the cliff, but Ana thought she knew differently.

She was responsible. Why else had she been sent to live with Mr Chan, an uncle who she hardly knew? A strange old man who kept his mouth shut and his head lowered, as if his eyes were deadly weapons, a man who rarely spoke except to fill her head with stories about the Soul Stealer . . .

Mr Chan ran the local supermarket around the corner from the school, where the bad girls used to hang out and steal stuff.

'It's easy,' they said, when they initiated younger girls into their gang. 'You can nick anything and he never sees you, because he hasn't got CCTV. He's scared of cameras. Thinks all those pictures are full of demons!'

When Poppy chased Ana with her N5000 camera phone, Ana froze with fear.

'Don't point that thief at me!' she shouted. 'Go away!'

'Thief?' Poppy sniggered. '*Thief!* Which century were you born in?' Then to the amusement of her cronies, Poppy articulated each word individually as if Ana couldn't understand. 'A *THIEF* STEALS CANDLESTICKS AND WALLETS. THIS IS A PHONE, ANA. UNDERSTAND? IT HAS A CAMERA INSIDE IT. YOU KNOW, *FLASH BANG WALLOP.* YOU *DO* KNOW WHAT A CAMERA IS, DON'T YOU?'

'Take that thief away!' Ana wailed.

'But I haven't stolen anything,' jeered Poppy.

'You don't know what Mr Chan has told me,' replied Ana. 'You will steal my soul.'

'Let's see, shall we?' said Poppy, pressing the button that clicked the shutter and flashed the flash in her eyeballs. Ana screamed and ran away. 'Don't you want your soul back?' Poppy mocked, holding her camera aloft like a trophy. The other girls crowded around in a froth of hysteria.

'Oh, Poppy!' they screeched. 'You are *so* funny!'

Carried away on this wave of adoration Poppy dismissed Ana as a screwball and used the camera to instigate a reign of terror in the playground. By starting a brand new sport that nobody else could play – Poppy's Photo Blackmail – she unleashed the bad girl inside of her!

> Did you know that there's bad inside everybody? They don't tell you, but it lives inside the appendix. That's why so many people have them cut out. And do you know where all those appendixes go? They give them to me. I store them in my freezer and when I want children to be even badder than they already are. I give them one to suck. like a lolly!

214

The first time Poppy played the blackmail game was in the school loos. She shoved her camera under the cubicle door and snapped a prefect on the pan.

'Oy! What's going on?' cried the victim.

'You have just been captured on my camera,' said Poppy, 'and unless you give me all the sweets in your pocket I shall put this photo on the noticeboard.'

'But everyone will see it,' cried the girl with no pants.

'Oh yes,' sniggered Poppy. 'I hadn't thought of that.' A crumpled paper bag full of sweets shot out under the door into Poppy's grasp. 'I hope you washed your hands!' she roared. 'Ha ha!'

During lunch, she hid behind the bike sheds and leaped out on a pair of secret lovers, interrupting their illicit kissing with a flash of her Nokisson.

'Oy! You two! That snog's going to cost you dear.'

The boy burst into tears when Poppy demanded his cap in return for not showing the photos to the head teacher. 'Please, Poppy,' he wailed. 'Don't tell anyone. I'm going out with Donna and if she finds

out I've been kissing another girl, she'll kill me.'

'That *is* Donna,' said Poppy.

'Is it?' said the boy, turning to the girl he'd just pulled. 'Are you Donna?'

'Yes,' she said. The boy looked confused.

'Who am I going out with then?'

✷ ✷ ✷

Poppy hung around the bus stop and caught her classmates copying homework off each other. She hooked her feet over the edge of the shelter roof, dropped down in front of them like a spider, and took an upside-down photograph of their cheating to hold them to account.

'Teacher's going to see what I've just seen,' she smirked. 'You are in such trouble.'

'You can't!' said the girl, whose homework the boy was copying.

'You wouldn't!' said the boy who hadn't been listening in class.

'I would and I could . . . but I won't,' said Poppy. 'Not if you do my homework for a year!'

The boy gasped. 'A year!'

'All right . . . two!' said Poppy. 'Say Hard Cheese!'

And she took a second photo just to rub it in.

✱ ✱ ✱

Over the next few weeks, Poppy used her camera to humiliate as many of her school friends as she could. It was a power trip. She loved the fact that she could control other people's lives and nobody could stop her. She loved it so much, in fact, that she extended her blackmailing to grown-ups.

This was her mistake. Some grown ups CAN be blackmailed; some CAN'T! Get it wrong at your peril!

Poppy blackmailed her mother first. She was in a field picking primroses when Poppy popped up from behind a tussock and digitally captured her on her phone.

'It's hardly a criminal offence,' her mother protested.

'I think you'll find that the Wildlife and Countryside Act of 1981 expressly forbids the picking of wild flowers. *You* might not think it's important, but there are several policemen who will.'

Her mother realised that she had been caught red-handed. 'What do you want this time?' she sighed.

'Full control over the TV remote on Tuesdays, Thursdays and Saturdays.'

For once Poppy's demands were not unreasonable. 'Fine,' said her mother, thinking she had got off lightly.

'And a holiday in Ibiza,' added Poppy slyly. 'Smile for the camera!'

Dippy mothers can be blackmailed.

Poppy caught her grandmother sneaking out of the Betting Shop having had a naughty flutter on *Lucky Pensioner* in the 3.30 at Rhyl.

'Poppy!' shrieked her granny, as the photograph was taken. 'You little sneak!'

'I'll take those winnings, Granny, unless you want me to report you to Gamblers Anonymous!' Then with no respect for age, she relieved her granny of ninety five pounds and ran off down the road to buy an iPod.

Lying grandmothers can be blackmailed.

Her fat father was a target too. He had been on a diet for as long as Poppy could

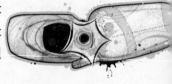

remember, yet despite her mother's best efforts he had never lost a pound. Her mother was baffled, but Poppy knew why. Every night her father would sneak downstairs and raid the fridge. All she had to do was wait and catch him with his snout in the trough!

Click. Poppy switched on her spotlight and lit up the fridge. Trapped in the shaft of light, Poppy's guilty father froze. In one hand he held a beer, in the other a pork pie and wedged between his teeth a chocolate orange.

'That snack's going to cost you big time, diet boy!' she said as she snapped his photo.

'It wasn't me!' he lied pathetically.

But Poppy stood her ground. 'The camera never lies, Dad. Mum will only see the truth.'

'OK,' he blubbed, scoffing the pork pie to comfort himself. 'What do you want this time?'

'I shall be filling that in with many excellent excuses,' she said, handing him a sheaf of letters. 'All you have to do is sign it.'

He read the one on top. '*Poppy cannot come to school today because* . . . Where's the rest of it?'

'That's down to you,' she said. 'You have to make up an excuse and then sign it. Aren't you proud of your little daughter, Daddy? There's one letter for every day of the school year!' If you can believe it, her father did as he was told and all for fear of his wife finding out that he was a midnight porker!

Feeble fathers can be blackmailed.

In case you hadn't gathered yet, Poppy's prying eye had turned her into a bully. But bullies always come a cropper. They never think they will but they always do.

They make the best guests too, because they are such big cowards. Tough in front of their friends, but put them in the Presidential Suite of Pain and they're all screams and pleadings to go home to mummy!

WHAT DID YOU SAY? SPEAK UP. I CAN'T HEAR YOU.

I said, it's semolina tonight, Jumbo. Your favourite.

* * *

The next day, Poppy spotted Ana in the street and ran across the road to block the younger girl's path.

'Hello, Ana,' she grinned as she slid the camera phone out of her pocket. 'I've come to steal your soul!'

Ana yelped and took off like a small Jack Russell. She slid through Poppy's legs, ran round the corner and dashed across the zebra-crossing into Mr Chan's supermarket. When Poppy caught up, Ana was hiding behind Mr Chan's legs. Poppy laughed contemptuously. He was not a tall man. In fact, he had a pigeon chest and a thin bony face. Not the sort of grown up to cause Poppy any trouble.

Or so she thought! Thin old shopkeepers called Mr Chan CAN'T be blackmailed!

'What do you want?' he said calmly, keeping his eyes fixed on the floor. 'No cameras allowed in here. Take that camera outside!' He pointed to the door.

'Why?' sneered Poppy. 'It's only a little snap.'

'If Ana says she does not want her picture taken, you must respect this.'

'You still haven't told me why,' jeered Poppy.

'Because she believes that the camera can kill a person by stealing their soul.'

'You've taught her this, have you?' said Poppy. 'It's a load of old rubbish!'

'Be careful what you say.' Mr Chan took hold of Poppy's arm and dragged her to one side. 'Ana's parents are dead,' he whispered. 'They died in an accident, slipping over a cliff, but she believes that they live on in her photographs. Ana is still little. She believes what she needs to believe to make her happy.'

'Well she needs to grow up,' sneered Poppy, 'because taking someone's photograph doesn't kill them.'

'It does if you take *this* man's photograph.' Mr Chan produced a battered photo from his pocket. It was a sepia print of an old Chinaman with wrinkled skin, long grey hair and a thin, bootlace moustache. 'He is powerful spirit what need to be fed. This is the Soul Stealer!'

'He looks so *un*scary!' shrieked Poppy. 'In fact he looks like you. Is it you?' She prodded Mr Chan in the shoulder.

'No!' shouted Ana all of a sudden. 'Don't do that.'

The old man did not flinch, but replied in a voice as cold as ice. 'If I am, know this. No one who takes a photograph of the Soul Stealer ever lives to take another. Now go, before it is too late.'

But Poppy was intrigued. 'I want to know what you're going to do to me if I take your photograph?' she said provocatively. 'Because it *is* you, isn't it? You're not telling me, but you are this Soul Stealer, aren't you?'

'He will take the life part of you and lock it into a picture for ever.'

'Oh yeah?' sniffed Poppy. 'So tell me this, oh wise uncle of the big cry-baby, how come the old bearded Chinaman who hates having his photo taken so much is in that photograph in your hand?'

'Because,' said Mr Chan in a calmly measured voice that sent a shiver down Poppy's spine, 'the man who took this photograph is now dead.'

Poppy laughed nervously. 'You mean the Soul Stealer, or should I say *you*, killed him just because you didn't like the picture?'

'Do not mock the Soul Stealer,' he warned, 'or he will steal your soul away. I suggest you leave now while you can still save your worthless bones!'

'You actually *believe* all this mumbo jumbo, don't you!' scoffed Poppy, raising the camera to her eye.

'Because it's TRUE!' screamed Ana, but her intervention came too late. Mr Chan looked up as Poppy pressed the button on her camera phone. As the flashlight exploded she saw something flicker in his eyes. They were camera shutters: diamond-shaped irises that opened and closed in the time it took him to blink.

* * *

Later that night, Poppy printed out her photographs. She was admiring her gallery of shame, as villains are wont to do, when she noticed something that made her blood run cold. In the photograph she had taken in the supermarket, Mr Chan's face had changed. The skin had wrinkled, the hair had grown long and grey and on the top lip sat a thin, bootlace moustache. It was the face of the Soul Stealer.

She looked through her other photographs and was horrified to see the same face staring back at her from the corner of each one. And alongside this face mysterious objects started to appear — dismembered body parts like the building bricks of a corpse. First a hand; then a hand and a foot; then a hand, a foot and a knee; then legs, arms and a torso. Suddenly there was the same headless figure in the bottom corner of each and every photograph. Even without a head she recognised it. It was *her*.

Now Poppy was nervous.

'What am I doing in my own photographs?' she trembled, jabbing her finger at the Soul Stealer. 'This is you, isn't it? This is your doing!'

The bootlace moustache twitched as the image stirred. 'I have stolen your soul!' it declared in a voice that roared, and sounded not unlike the voice of Mr Chan.

In horror, Poppy watched as *her* head materialised on top of the headless figures. In the picture, she had a digital camera pressed to her eye and her mouth was moving. 'Watch the birdie, me!' said her photographic self. There was a flash as Poppy took her own photograph. Then she was gone, leaving the room cold and empty.

Ana never saw Poppy again. Poppy's parents never saw Poppy again either. Not in the flesh. A few days later, her mother found a copy of the black and white photograph behind the fridge.

'How did this get here?' she exclaimed. 'I haven't

seen this photograph for years. Look, George!'
Poppy's father raised his head from his su-doku
puzzle.

'Is that the photograph of us at primary school
together?' he asked.

'Yes,' said Poppy's mother. As she peered more
closely at the image, her voice suddenly
trembled and faltered. 'I don't remember
Poppy being there, do you?'

'She wasn't born,' he said. Which, of
course, she wasn't.

Yet there she was in full-blown colour.
Poppy's stolen soul had been torn from the
living world and sent to live in that black
and white photograph for ever. And *that*, in
case you hadn't worked it out for yourself, is
why she's always crying!

Of course I should point out that the photograph
the parents have is only a copy. The REAL
photograph in which the real Poppy is imprisoned
lives down here in The Darkness . . . in a shoebox,
in the spidery attic where creeping damp and mould
can slowly do its worst on the paper. By my
reckoning Poppy has another ninety-three years to
live before she is entirely consumed by mildew!

Aaaaaaaaaaaagh! This is a nightmare!

Welcome to the Darkness. Nobby

I've saved the MOST GRUESOME GROWN-UPS till last. It's not that they're evil. It's just that they're a GRUESOME SIGHT! This is because there is rather a lot of unnecessary nudity in this story. Because of this adult content I'm afraid I must ask you to sign the disclaimer below. just to cover me in the event of your parents catching you reading the story and wanting to take me to court. There's NO NEED TO READ the disclaimer. It's all PERFECTLY ABOVE BOARD. JUST SIGN IT and let's get on. It's nothing more than a completely HARMLESS STATEMENT saying that it's not my fault if you find the story a bit too rude and die of shock. Honest.

Thank you very much!

DISCLAIMER
I WON'T CAUSE TROUBLE!

If you use this disclaimer as a donor card and my signature as

proof that I donate my body and all its contents be it whole or in

several little bits to the Hothell Darkness.

SIGNED: *(In blood, please)*

....

227

The worst thing about dreams is that sometimes you can't tell where the dreaming stops and real life begins. You're lying in the bath when a red-hot buzz saw drops through the ceiling and spins towards your skull. Is it real or are you dreaming? Should you move out of its way or let it slice through your brain? And if you let it chop your brain into slivers of salami will you live to regret it when you get the call to appear on Mastermind? Is your father a spaceman? Does your mother have a tail? And are those real vampire teeth in your teacher's mouth or plastic ones? When you can't tell the difference, life becomes just that little bit more problematic.

NOBBY'S NIGHTMARE

Nobby's problems began when he was walking out with the girl of his dreams. After much discussion, they had decided not to feed the ducks and go to the cinema instead. Their hearts were pounding as they strolled through the busy pedestrian precinct holding hands in a rather self-conscious way. They wanted everyone to think that they held hands all the time, which would make today no big deal, but that was a lie. This was a first and both their hands were sweaty.

'All right, Sophie?' he said.

'All right, Nobby!' she replied, removing the chewing gum from her mouth and sticking it to the trunk of a tree.

'Having a good time?'

'Luvly!' She unwrapped another piece of chewing gum and popped it in her mouth. Then she screwed up the paper and dropped it on the ground. 'Here,' she said casually. 'I haven't lost my clothes too, have I?'

'What?' Nobby's heart stopped as he looked down and saw pink. 'Oh nuts! I'm naked!' But that was not all. Out of the corner of his eye he realised that Sophie had changed too. She was green and knobbly. 'Aaagh!' he screamed. 'And you've turned into an alien.'

'Of course I have,' she said, hitching her wide, flat bottom over her knees so that she could walk. 'An alien's the only thing in the universe that would walk out with a rudey-nudey like you.'

'But I can't go out with someone who's green,' panicked Nobby, horribly aware of the warts and calluses that had suddenly appeared on Sophie's hand.

'You liked me a minute ago,' she said, clinging on to his fingers as he tried to disentangle them from hers.

'People will laugh!' he cried, as passers-by stopped and stared.

'Oh dear. Well if you can't see beyond my skin colour,' she said, turning to face him. 'I'm afraid I'm going to have to eat you.'

'What? NO!' Nobby's heart pounded in his ears while inside his head a loud voice yelled

'Wake up! Wake up!' As Sophie drew back her lips and flashed a row of fearsomely sharp teeth, Nobby pinched himself all over. 'I can't feel a thing!' he wailed. 'This must be real.'

'Sorry!' smiled Sophie, lunging towards him like a giant grain-pecking chicken on steroids.

Nobby put his arms in front of his face to fend her off. 'NO!' he screamed. 'NO!' But her blunt beak was too powerful. 'Aaaaaagh!'

And then he woke up.

'Wuh!' He sat up in bed with sweat beading his top lip. Sophie really *was* the girl of his dreams.

His bad ones!

Whenever he dreamed about her, which was all the time, he always ended up naked. He'd been to see dream doctors about what these dreams meant, but they'd all offered the same interpretation . . . that Nobby clearly *wanted* to be naked with Sophie and his dream was a manifestation of that. But Nobby knew this to be bunkum. He knew the real reason why he always ended up in the buff. It was his parents. They were to blame. They were to blame for everything!

231

Just then, the bedroom door opened and Nobby's parents walked in. His dad was carrying a comic that he'd just ironed and his mother was carrying a tray full of food. Both of them were naked – their bits were hanging out for the entire world to see.

'Morning, Nobby,' said his father, opening the curtains with a flourish.

'Brought your breakfast,' said his mother, placing the tray on top of Nobby's legs. 'Two boiled eggs today.'

'And a buttered soldier,' added his father, laying the comic on the duvet.

Nobby's parents were naturists.

For as long as Nobby could remember, his parents had embarrassed him with their hairy hobby. They had joined a naturist club when he was still in his pram. In those days they took him with them, but when he stopped needing a nappy he refused to go. It curled his toes to sit in the games room and watch his parents playing ping-pong and rummicub in the raw. In fact, as far as Nobby was concerned, *everything* at that naturist club was unnatural. They had a cinema where they watched films in the nude, they had shops where they shopped in the nude and they had barbecues where they cooked in the nude. And when there was a fancy-dress party they did that in the nude as well. Only everyone went as the same two people.

Helpful Hints on How To Deal With Gruesome Grown-Ups

4. IF YOUR PARENTS ARE NATURISTS . . .

Break the tumble dryer and buy an industrial mangle. Then while your father is turning the handle and your mother is feeding your clothes through the rollers, fire a pebble at their bare cheeks with a catapult. They will leap forward and catch their bits in the mangle, and with bits as mangled as that they will never want to show them in public again!

'No don't tell me. Let me guess who you've come as. Is it Adam and Eve?'

What made Nobby's life even worse, however,

was that his parents didn't wear clothes at home, either. Nobby was fed up with sharing the sofa with his parents' rolls of fat, and there was something not entirely savoury about eating a pork pie with your father's bellybutton winking at you over the top of the table.

'There's nothing wrong with taking your clothes off in the privacy of your own home,' his mother said repeatedly. 'Everyone's the same underneath, Nobby.'

'Not true,' he said, checking out her dimpled bottom. 'Some of us are a bit lumpier.'

✳ ✳ ✳

Thanks to Nobby's awful parents Nobby's life was a nightmare. He had no friends, because every time one of his schoolmates came round to ask Nobby out, they had to run the gruesome gauntlet of wobbly pink bits. It didn't matter whether the bits were wobbling behind the vacuum cleaner or swinging behind the lawn mower, it was still a horrible sight, and once they'd copped an eyeful Nobby's friends never came back. Little wonder then that Nobby longed to be rid of his parents. With them gone, his life would be normal and he could finally ask Sophie round.

***

Then one day, Nobby's living nightmare took an unexpected twist. He came down for breakfast to find his parents standing in the hall with their clothes *on*.

'We're going out,' said his mother. 'We're taking a bus to the naturist club.' Thankfully, that was one thing his parents never did. Hit the streets naked.

'It's an afternoon of Nude Olympics!' explained his father. 'Why don't you come?'

'Oh go on,' said his mother. 'It's going to be such fun.'

But there was not a bone in Nobby's body that shared her enthusiasm. 'I'm busy,' he sneered. 'Wearing clothes and being normal.'

'You'll be here all on your own if you don't come,' she added, thinking that being on his own would put Nobby off. It hadn't crossed her mind that it might appeal to him. And it did, because this was the opportunity that Nobby had been waiting for. This was the chance to put his master plan into operation.

***

He secretly followed them to the naturist club, waited until they were inside, had stripped off and were playing badminton with a bearded couple called the Hendersons, then sneaked in and stole every piece of clothing on site. With nothing of their own, or anyone else's to wear, Nobby's parents were now trapped inside the club for ever. They couldn't get home unless they walked down the street or went on a bus in the nude, and even *they* weren't prepared to do that! His plan had worked. His life was finally free from embarrassment. Nobby's nightmare was over!

Now that he could do what he liked, he phoned up Sophie and said in his sexiest voice, 'All right, Sophie?'

'All right, Nobby!' she replied.

'Having a good time?' he said.

'Luvly!'

'Doing anything tonight?'

'Washing my hair.'

'Fancy going out?'

'With you?'

'Yeah.'

'Sure,' she said. And Nobby, not unreasonably, thought that *that* was that.

> What Nobby didn't know was that nightmares are never over! Like Great White Sharks they just dive under the surface for a bit then come back up when you're least expecting it and bite your head off! That's the beauty of nightmares; they never stop and you never know when you're in one!

Nobby was just putting the phone down when he heard Sophie still talking on the other end of the line. He lifted the receiver back to his ear. 'Sorry,' he said. 'What did you say?'

'I said I'll bring my parents round to meet your parents tonight then.'

'What?' he gasped. 'You want *your* parents to meet *my* parents?'

'I can't go out with you if they don't like you and your family!' she said.

But he didn't *have* any parents. He'd just got rid of them. This was unbelievable timing. Seconds away from pulling the girl of his dreams and suddenly she wants to meet his parents who weren't there! This couldn't be happening to him. He clutched at his chest where a stabbing pain was tearing through his ribs. Oh great! Now he was having a heart attack!

And that was when he woke up.

'Wuh!' He was in the sitting room in an armchair. 'Yes!' he cried with relief. 'I was dreaming! She doesn't want her parents to meet mine after all! Yes! It was just a bad dream! YES!'

But then he looked around the room and saw his parents sitting on the sofa opposite him. They would have been naked had it not been for the saucepans that were strategically placed over their rude bits.

'NO!' howled Nobby. 'What are *you* doing here?

'You came and fetched us,' said his mother. 'Most inconvenient timing it was too.'

'No, I didn't!' protested Nobby. 'That was in my dream.' His eyes lit up suddenly. 'That's it!' he yelled. 'I'm dreaming this as well, aren't I? Please,' he begged. 'Tell me you're just figments of my imagination.'

'You said there was an emergency,' she continued. 'You told us to drop our shuttlecocks and come right away.'

'Only some joker had nicked our clothes,' said Nobby's father. 'So you gave us these saucepans and brought us home on the bus.'

'You told us we had to meet

your girlfriend's parents,' said his mother.

Nobby pinched himself hard. 'You mean this is really happening?' he said. 'Then why can't I feel anything?' He frantically punched the top of his arm as the doorbell rang.

'That'll be them!' he squeaked. 'They're here.'

'Aren't you going to answer it?' asked his mother, straightening the magazines on the coffee table.

'No,' snapped Nobby. Then, 'Yes. No. OK! But whatever happens, be normal and keep those saucepans on!'

'We're not ashamed of our bodies,' said his father.

'No,' said Nobby, 'but I am.'

* * *

In the hall, Nobby checked his face in the mirror hoping to find proof that he was still in the middle of a nightmare. Did he have horns, for example, or a forked tongue or pixie ears? Sadly, everything was normal. That meant Sophie really *was* outside with her parents, and *had* been for several minutes. He took a deep breath and opened the front door.

'Hello, everyone,' he said breezily, trying to act

as naturally as he could.

'Where've you been?' snapped Sophie. 'We've been standing out here for ages.'

'So sorry,' cringed Nobby, smiling at the unsmiling adults standing behind his would-be girlfriend. 'Mum and dad were cooking – and, you know how these things happn – they just fell into some saucepans.'

'Nobby!' said Sophie curtly. The tone of her voice told him that he was talking too much. 'These are my parents. Lord and Lady Pinkerton.'

'Lord and Lady . . . Oh . . .' Nobby had no idea they were titled! Now that he looked at them – *his* tweed suit and monocle; *her* blue cardigan and pearls – he could see quite clearly that they were nobs.

'I do hope you're a straight kind of family,' barked Lord Pinkerton in his no nonsense, let's-have-less-of-this-shilly-shallying voice.

'Weirdos won't do for our Soph,' added his wife with gusto.

'No,' blushed Nobby. 'Absolutely not.' All he could think about was his excruciating parents sitting in the other room wearing nothing but saucepans. 'Umm . . . Do come in.'

When they walked into the sitting room, Nobby's parents were sitting down.

'Lord and Lady Pinkerton,' gulped Nobby, 'these are my parents.'

Unfortunately for Nobby, his parents had old-fashioned manners. When Lord Pinkerton offered his hand, Nobby's parents stood up and offered theirs.

'Delighted to meet you,' they said as the saucepans clattered to the floor, leaving both-stark-bottom naked!

Nobby screamed and punched his arm again. 'Wake up! Wake up! Wake up!' he yelled, but nothing doing. This was no dream. 'Why are you so embarrassing?' he wailed.

'Who's embarrassed?' said Lady Pinkerton. 'I'm not. My husband's not. Sophie?'

'No,' said the girl of his dreams.

Nobby was gobsmacked. 'You're not embarrassed by my naked parents?' he gasped.

'You should see what my parents look like under their clothes,' laughed Sophie. Up until that moment, Nobby could just about cope, but now . . .

'No. No. No. No. No! They're not going to take their clothes off as well, are they?' Before he had even finished his sentence he had his answer. 'Oh good gracious, they ARE!' Without any show of surprise from their daughter, Lord and Lady Pinkerton peeled off their clothes and their portly flesh sprang unfettered into the room.

Nobody but Nobby seemed to notice that there were two green aliens with tails, blunt beaks and saggy baggy bellies standing in their sitting room. His naked parents were shaking their guests' flippers and smiling politely.

'We're from the planet Boobletrox,' said the alien formerly known as Lord Pinkerton, 'where naturism is the norm.'

'I can't tell you what a pleasure it is to get those body suits off,' his wife trilled. 'It's the first time since we landed on earth that we don't have to pretend we're somebody we're not. Close your mouth, Nobby dear.'

Nobby's mouth had fallen open with surprise. 'And now that you've met us properly,' announced Sophie's father, 'you have our permission to go out with Sophie.'

Suddenly, Nobby wasn't so sure he wanted to. If the parents were both aliens that made *her* an alien too. Either that or this was another bad dream. He dug his fingernails into the palms of both hands, kicked his own shins and twisted his ear lobes, but nothing woke him up. This was REAL.

'OK,' said Sophie. 'I will go out with Nobby on a trial date, but only on one condition. If *I* have to go naked, so must *he*.'

Now Nobby was really lost. 'What do you mean "go naked"?'

❋ ❋ ❋

Half an hour later, Nobby's real life was bizarrely imitating his dreams. He and Sophie were strolling through the busy pedestrian precinct holding hands in a rather self-conscious way. He was completely naked, while she had discarded her human form and was waddling along beside him in that menacing way that makes green aliens so scary.

'Stop fidgeting,' she hissed. 'Nobody's looking at *you*. They're all staring at *me*.' Nobby pulled his hand out of her flipper and hid behind a lamppost.

'This is a dream!' he cried. 'Wake up! Wake up! WAKE UP!' But everything he did to wake himself up just hurt.

'Of course it hurts,' said
Sophie. 'Because all of this is
real.'

'It can't be real,' blubbed Nobby. 'This is my worst
nightmare. I mean being naked in the street with a
hungry alien is . . .' He stopped as a really bad
memory resurfaced in his head. 'Oh no! I know
what's going to happen next!'

'What?'

'You're going to eat me!'

'Eat you!' Sophie laughed, wetting her beak with
the tip of her short black tongue. 'Why would I eat
you?' But even as she spoke Nobby knew he was in
trouble. Her eyes had suddenly lit up in a way they
never had for him. 'Oh look who it is!' she
gasped, pointing to a handsome boy who
was admiring himself in a shop window on
the other side of the street. 'It's Luke Loveaduck.
He mustn't see me with you . . .' Nobby was
appalled.

'Why not?!' he said. 'I'm your date!'

'In your dreams,' replied Sophie. 'because if
he *does* see me with you, he'll think I'm
a loser.'

'A loser?'

'Yes. With no taste in men. And he'll never ask me out.' This date with Sophie was turning into a worse nightmare than Nobby's worst nightmare. 'Sorry!' she smiled, lunging towards him like a giant grain-pecking chicken on steroids. Nobby put his arms in front of his face to fend her off.

'NO!' he screamed. 'NO!' But her blunt beak was too powerful. She ate him up with a crunch, a squirt and a bursting eyeball, and as if that wasn't bad enough she then turned back into Sophie and waved at the boy across the street in a rather obvious, I'm-currently-available way!

'Yoo hoo,' she cried. 'Luke! Over here!'

And then he woke up!

'Wuh!' Nobby had never been so relieved to discover that everything had just been a terrible dream. His date with Sophie had been so profoundly depressing that he knew it couldn't have been real. Grown-ups *weren't* aliens. Girls *didn't* suddenly turn into green monsters with the appetite to eat a whole boy!

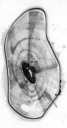He yawned, but could only open his lips a short way. His mouth was covered in sticky

goo. His eyes were half closed as well, like a newborn baby's. He wasn't quite sure where he was either. He could hear gurgling like an underground stream and distant explosions of gas, like a car backfiring. He rubbed his eyes and cleared away the film.

'Oh!'

Nobby had never been inside an alien's stomach before with its storms of acid rain, its grinding stone walls and its little farty geysers, but since his first nightmare he'd *thought* about it often, and this was exactly what he had imagined it would look like. Which only goes to prove that it was all real and you should never judge a person by the colour of their skin. Some green aliens can be nice, whereas others can eat you. It's just luck, really.

Sweet dreams and don't have nightmares!

Now that you've read everyone's stories is it any clearer why I want you to come and live down here in The Darkness? It's not for me. It's for YOU. Grown-ups are so mean it's NOT SAFE for you up there. If you don't get down here now, how will you know that your mother isn't filling the shampoo bottle with sulphuric acid, or that the milkman isn't lacing your milk with cyanide, or that the new barber doesn't have knives instead of fingers and a no-nonsense way of trimming your head from your shoulders?

You can't know. So don't take the risk.

Come along. It's time to go now. Leave a note for your parents, pack pyjamas and a teddy and let's have no more delay.

OK. let's go. Just lock your bedroom door first so your parents can't barge in and stop us.

I said. 'LOCK THE DOOR!' NOT 'STEP THROUGH IT